AF420025

OUTLAWS PUBLISHING

Wind River
Mountain Man Jeb Winslow

DAVID W. BAILEY

For information contact: info@outlawspublishing.com

Cover Art by Michael Thomas
Cover design by Outlaws Publishing LLC
Published by Outlaws Publishing LLC
February 2021
10 9 8 7 6 5 4 3 2 1

Prologue

When Wyoming was designated as a territory in the spring of 1868 and John A. Campbell was appointed territorial governor, not long afterwards in the Wind River Valley, the Sioux raided a camp where four white men were killed and numerous horses and mules were stolen. When the raid had come to the attention of the county authorities, they reported it to the territorial governor, who in turn requested military support and protection for the settlers in that area. The Army sent two companies of Cavalry to the area. Since Fort Bridger was close to 200 miles away, the Army established Camp Nelson, and supplies were much needed to combat the Sioux uprising along the Wind River, thus the, 'Wind River Campaign' had begun.

The commander at Fort Bridger sent supplies of weapons and ammunition by wagon train to Camp Nelson to try and squelch the Indian uprisings and arm the settlers against Indian attacks. This strategy worked, but only for a short time. Then, later that month, the Sioux struck again, this time, a mining settlement four miles east of the town of Beaver falls. Again, four white men were killed, and numerous horses and mules were stolen. The Sioux were then chased away by the Army stationed at Camp Nelson. Then, the Sioux struck again two days later. The Sioux attacked three men who were traveling on the road near the Popo Agie River, at the North Fork of the Big Wind River.

CHAPTER ONE

Cedar Creek

All seemed quiet. Not a sound of ill wind. Jeb Winslow, Lex Turner and Brent Jacoby were traveling on the road near the Popo Agie River, at the North Fork of the Big Wind River. These men were trappers and fur traders, and they had a huge haul of furs to sell or trade. These men had three pack horses and two mules loaded down with all manner of furs, beaver pelts, supplies and goods to barter with when they reached the town of Beaver Falls. As they rode abreast of each other, each man was joyously telling the other what he had in mind when they had some coin, to do a little jig, a jug, and a woman to help him do both, he would be a happy man. In the telling, each man had the same idea in mind, but a little different than the other.

Then, an arrow stuck in the chest of Lex Turner with a thud. Surprised, he grabbed the shaft of the arrow, slumped in the saddle, then wide eyed, he slid from the saddle to the ground. The Sioux screamed a war cry as Jeb Winslow and Brent Jacoby went for their weapons, but before they could defend themselves, the Sioux were all over them. After being wrestled from their horses, a hand to hand scuffle ensued. Brent Jacoby was killed and Jeb Winslow was wounded, but played dead. The Sioux, believing that all three men were dead, took their pack horses, mules and all their supplies, plus their weapons.

When Jeb Winslow finally came around, he tried to sit up, but found it too difficult. He lay there, breathing erratically, eyes moving and ears listening. After a few minutes, he tried to sit up again, but this time, he sat up through the pain. He moaned mournfully as his head throbbed and his body ached. He swayed in the sitting position as his eyes went blurry. He closed his eyes and balanced himself with his hands on the ground at both sides. It took a few minutes for his head to stop spinning and his eyes to gain clarity. He felt something running down the left side of his face. He reached up to find out and brought back blood on his hand. He sat looking around at his friends who lay dead. He knew he had to walk because the horses were gone. He sighed heavily as he tried to come to his feet. Groggily, he sat back down. Then, everything went dark as he fell over onto his right side. He had passed out.

When he finally came to again, he found himself on a wagon full of supplies. There were weapons, ammunition, and various food supplies as well as tack. He ventured to sit up. This time, it wasn't too difficult. He noticed a couple of troopers in the driver seat and wearily crawled over some crates of supplies to ask where he was. The troopers were surprised at his being awake and said as much. A trooper told him he was in a supply train headed for Camp Nelson with much needed supplies. He estimated Camp Nelson was at least ten miles away.

Jeb then asked, "how about my two friends? Did you...?"

One trooper replied, "yes, we buried 'em. You're lucky you ain't dead yourself, Mister."

Jeb replied, "all's I can say is, someone up there likes me."

The same trooper then said, "well, it's lucky for you we came along when we did, or you'd be walkin' right about now and dead on your feet. No pun intended."

Jeb replied, "thanks for the ride, and for what ya did for my friends. I do appreciate that."

The same trooper said, "no thanks needed, Mister...?"

"Winslow. Jeb Winslow. Trapper, fur trader extraordinaire. Me and my friends had a huge haul of furs and beaver pelts until them Sioux took everything, leavin' me the only one breathin'."

"You're dang lucky they didn't lift your hair as well, Mister Winslow. They must've been in a real big hurry to forgit somethin' like that."

"I'm right glad they did. Say, how long have I been on this wagon, anyways?" He settled himself down between two crates of supplies just behind the driver's seat.

"A day and a half, I reckon," came the reply.

"That long, huh?" he asked. "That injun must've hit me purdy hard for me to do something like this. I've had my bell rung a few times, let me tell ya, but nothin' compared to this."

The same trooper replied, "well, those war clubs ain't nothin' to sneeze at. He must've just grazed ya when he swung that thing at ya."

"It sure don't feel like he did. By the way, who patched me up? I can feel the bandages."

"That would be Miss Porter," the trooper answered. "She's on her way to meet up with her fiancé at Camp Nelson. Maybe ya know him? His name is Lieutenant Paul Landers."

"Landers, huh," he said. "Nope, don't know him. I'll be thankin' her when next we stop."

"Won't be too long now," the trooper replied. "Pert near dusk. We'll be stoppin' at Cedar Creek, most likely. Onliest closest place there is. There's good water there. Cool, clear and refreshin'. 'Sides, need to have that bandage replaced with a clean one."

"Is she purdy?" Jeb asked.

"Is who purdy?" asked the trooper.

"Miss Porter," Jeb answered.

The trooper replied, "oh. Yep, she sure is. Purdier'n a speckled pup. She sure is."

"Ain't that somethin'?" Jeb replied. "Been a while since I seen a purdy gal, or any gal for that matter. Been trappin' since last winter, me and..." He sighed, then said, "it's real hard to think of my friends in the past tense of the word." He paused, then said, "I'll be a payin' them Injuns back soon enough alright. I doubt I git my furs back, or even the horses and the mules, but scalps will do for now."

Silence permeated the wagon as Jeb rested his weary head against the oiled tarp of the wagon. The rocking of the wagon soon put him to sleep. The jostling of the wagon seemed to put more weariness in Jeb's eyes, for he was snoring loud enough to build his own log cabin. Two story at that. Yes, sir, he was dead to the world. No pun intended. The only thing that woke him was the sudden stop. He shook out the weariness and called out to the driver, asking, "trouble?"

The driver replied, "nah. Camp for the night, Mister Winslow. Cedar Creek."

Soon, the campfire was lit and coffee on to boil. Johnny cake was in Dutch ovens and beans were above the fire in a pot on a roasting rod. The trooper was quite correct. Miss Porter was a very handsome woman and Jeb looked on her in respect and delight. As she unwound the bloody bandage from his head, he stared at her admiringly.

She asked, "see somethin' you like, Mister Winslow?"

"Oh, yes, Ma'am," he replied. "I surely do. 'Course, I know it ain't proper, me lookin' at you like this, it's just,

I haven't seen a purdy gal in quite some time, and if you ain't the purdiest one ever I did see, too."

"Thank you, Mister Winslow," she replied. "How kind."

Jeb then said, "ah, you can quit that mister stuff. The name's Jeb. You can call me that, if'n ya'd like."

As she was inspecting his head wound, she said, "you do know I have a fiancé? I'm on my way to meet him at Camp Nelson."

Oh, yes, Ma'am," he answered. "That was explained to me a while ago. I must say, this feller you're gonna meet is one lucky so and so, if'n you don't mind me sayin'."

"His name happens to be..."

Jeb interrupted her, saying, "Lieutenant Paul Landers. Yes'm. I know."

"Well, Mister, I mean, Jeb, you will have a scar, I'm afraid."

Jeb replied, "oh, that's alright. The company I keep, we call that character."

"Well, the company I keep, we call it a scar." She smiled. "Let's just put a little salve on it and rebandage it, and you'll be fit as a fiddle in just a few days or so."

"You have the gentlest touch ever I felt. You'd make a down right dandy nurse, if'n that's to your likin'."

"Well, Jeb," she replied, "that was my calling before I met Paul. I lived in Upstate New York and worked at Saint Mary's Hospital for the blind and invalid. There was just too many after the war, but it was steady work."

"And, this Paul took you away from all that, did he?" Jeb asked.

"Not really, no," she answered. "I took myself away from all that. Paul did say I could keep up with my work there, but I found being a nurse as well as a wife, I had too many duties to keep track of, trying to handle those duties myself." She finished wrapping his head with a fresh bandage and smiled. "There. That ought to hold you for a while."

"I surely do thank you, Miss Porter. I purely do."

"Miss Porter is too fancy. Just call me Linda." She smiled.

"Well, Linda," Jeb replied, "I do thank you for what you've done for me."

Linda then replied, "it's what I was trained to do, Jeb, albeit behind me now."

"To my way of thinkin', that's a shame," Jeb said. "Seems to me, that kinda trainin' not bein' done, is a waste of trainin'."

She replied, "my choice, Jeb."

"Can't argue that, Linda, but it's such a waste. You have kind and gentle hands." Jeb then remarked, "that

Johnny cake sure do smell good. A cup of coffee smells really good, too." He paused, then said, "How 'bout we not dilly dally and put on the feed bag, huh?"

Linda chuckled, then replied, "sounds good to me, too."

"Well, then, let's git to it, shall we?"

The camp was abuzz with activity and alive with chit chat. Then, the commanding officer of the supply wagons came over to where Jeb was seated on a downed tree limb. "Well, Mister Winslow, how are you?"

"As well as could be expected, Lieutenant," Jeb answered, and took another bite of his Johnny cake covered in beans.

"I'm Lieutenant Jirus Brentwood. We thought for a while there, you weren't going to be with us much longer. That was a nasty head wound. Sioux, I take it?"

"And you'd be right, Lieutenant," answered Jeb. "Killed my two friends. I was wounded, and them red devils took everything we worked hard for since last winter."

Lieutenant Brentwood said, "that's tough. I'm sorry to hear that."

Jeb replied, "they'll git their comeuppance, once I git back on my feet. Once I have a horse under me and weapons to deal with 'em, I'll git my revenge, but quick."

The Lieutenant said, "Well, we'll be in Camp Nelson around noon tomorrow, so we'll see about putting a horse under you, but the weapons will be your own worry. And, I wouldn't be going up against the Sioux without backup, and that wouldn't be enough. Just let the Army handle the Sioux."

Jeb gave the lieutenant a hard stare, then said, "I lost two good friends because of the Sioux, Lieutenant. Very good friends. You don't let that go too lightly, without wantin' revenge."

"I understand that, Mister Winslow," Lieutenant Brentwood replied, "but the Army is here to keep the peace in whatever manner it sees fit, and if that means curtailing your efforts for revenge against the Sioux, then so be it."

Jeb replied, matter-of-factly, "then, Lieutenant, I say we see things differently."

"It's true the Army is also here to protect the settlers in this area, but we are not here to let you settle a blood feud, causing more attacks from the Sioux."

Jeb replied, "they surely don't need my help in that, now do they? They're all stirred up like bees in a hive about us bein' here in the first place, and you Army boys ain't makin' it any better."

"We were sent here to do a job, Mister Winslow, and like it or not, that's just what we plan to do, and we don't need your approval in doing it, either."

"Well, Lieutenant," Jeb said, "don't let me keep you from doin' your duty as you see it. Leave me to mine and we'll both be happy."

"Then, we understand each other, Mister Winslow." Lieutenant Brentwood then said, "enjoy your meal."

"Can't," Jeb replied, as he set his plate aside. "Lost my appetite."

Lieutenant Brentwood remarked, "it was Army grub, so I didn't think you'd like it anyways."

Jeb stood to his feet. "Well, Lieutenant, it looks as though we're gonna have a go at each other sooner or later, huh? If you don't stop badgerin' me, it'll surely happen. As sure as you're born."

"Looks like, Winslow, but let's wait 'til your wound heals before that happens."

"Why wait when we can git'r done right here and now?"

"We'll wait, Winslow. It just wouldn't be a fair fight at this point. The way you are now, you'd surely lose."

"Well, you just let me worry 'bout that, Lieutenant," Jeb replied as he took a stance to engage in fisticuffs. "Let's get after it."

At that said, Lieutenant Brentwood turned and walked away.

"Hmph!" Jeb scoffed. "You afraid of me or somethin'?"

"Hardly that, Winslow," Lieutenant Brentwood replied over his shoulder. He then turned to face Jeb. "Afraid of hurting you more than what you already are."

Dropping his hands, Jeb said, "your concern for my health just now just brings me to tears."

"Don't flatter yourself, Winslow." Lieutenant Brentwood turned and walked away.

Soon, the camp was quiet, except for the wood burning in the camp fire. The crackling and popping of the wood from the heat seemed to calm the nerves of those in camp. An owl, not far from camp, began to hoot, 'hoo, hoo.' The night birds began to sing to each other and the bullfrogs joined in the noise and began to croak. Grasshoppers chirping. All these noises in the night was an alarm system. They would stop if danger lurked nearby. Then suddenly, they stopped.

Jeb had been awake, listening to the night sounds, and came fully erect in his bedroll. He reached for a weapon and realized he had none. He quickly and quietly came to his feet, then went to wake Lieutenant Brentwood with what might be a possible attack from whoever is out there.

Groggily, Lieutenant Brentwood stirred and asked what the matter was.

Jeb quietly replied, "I smell Injuns, Lieutenant." He paused then said, "listen." As he looked around the area with his head high, he added, "too quiet."

The lieutenant sat up on his bedroll and listened, then whispered, "wake the camp quietly, Winslow. We must meet and repel the Indians, if that is in fact who they are."

"Injuns, I tell ya," Jeb said. "I can smell 'em, and they're close."

After waking Lieutenant Brentwood, he and the lieutenant knew what to do. He and Jeb quietly woke the camp. Every man dressed quickly and quietly, then armed themselves.

It was four o'clock in the morning by then. Then Jeb was given a rifle to protect himself. As he took the rifle, he realized it was a sixteen round, .44 caliber rimfire, breech-loading, lever action Henry repeating rifle. He smiled widely as he loaded his pockets with 44.40 caliber ammunition, then took to cover behind a large downed tree limb. He levered a round in the chamber and waited. The coolness of the morning air kept the sweat from their brows, but their nerves and senses were on high alert at the nearest sound. The bushes being rustled, a twig snapping. If there was a rooster any where's about, it would have crowed by now. Then, a Whippoorwill sounded off to the left of the camp. Seconds later, it was answered from somewhere off to the right side of the camp.

At each sounding, all heads turned in the direction of the sound. Expectations rose in the camp, waiting for what was to come. As the sun rose over the mountains, there came a war cry. Then, the Indians came rushing into the camp, firing their weapons and shooting arrows at the troopers. It was the Sioux making another raid. The Indians were met with heavy rifle fire from every point in the camp. Indians began falling from their ponies. A couple troopers doubled over and fell on their faces. The noise was deafening and thunderous that left the ears ringing. Gun smoke filled the air as the Indians raced on horseback, one way, then the other. A few Indians jumped from their ponies to attack on foot but were swiftly dispatched.

Then, they were gone, for the moment, leaving the ground littered with the dead and dying. Lieutenant Brentwood and Jeb came from cover, looking at the human cost of that attack. Lieutenant Brentwood still holding his smoking side arm. Numerous Sioux dead and dying. Five troopers dead, two wounded. Then, whooshing sounds came to their ears.

Jeb yelled out, "flaming arrows!"

Lieutenant Brentwood turned to see a supply wagon get hit with a flaming arrow and the tarp began to burn, then another. "Put those fires out. There's guns and ammo in those wagons. It'll be like hell fire if that ammo explodes!"

Troopers began to scramble getting water to put out the fires, only to hurry to remove the tarps and let them burn on the ground. During the removal of the tarps, the Sioux used this time to pick off one or two troopers. The flaming arrows continued, striking wagons, as well as troopers, as they ran for water. There was chaos and fear in the camp as the flaming arrows continued to rain down on them.

Jeb had taken up a position near a large boulder and knelt by it, levering another round in the chamber. "I'm waitin' for ya, you red devils! Come and git a dose of lead poisonin'!" He yelled out, laughing almost maniacally.

Then, an arrow landed next to him with a thwack as it stuck in the ground. He turned, raised his rifle, and fired. An Indian who came running at him with knife in hand, was turned sideways by the impact of the bullet, falling on his right side, then rolling onto his back. Again, Jeb laughed almost maniacally as he levered another round in the chamber.

Again he yelled, "ya missed! Come and git me, you sons of Satan!"

Then a woman screamed. Jeb realized who it was. Linda Porter. He quickly rose to his feet and took off running. He found her being wrestled away by two Indians. She was sure putting up a struggle, but Jeb knew she didn't stand a chance against warriors who were stronger than she was.

He shot one of the Indians, but was unable to fire a second time. The warrior released his grip on Linda then was quickly on Jeb like a shirt. They tumbled to the ground, pushing and pulling at each other. Linda stood screaming at the two as they wrestled with each other. They bit, pulled hair, kicked and gouged each other as the dirt was kicked up from their tussle.

Then they separated and Jeb lunged at the Indian. The warrior grabbed Jeb's hands and fell backwards, dragging Jeb with him, and then kicked him over his shoulder. Jeb landed on his back as the Indian quickly came to his feet. Turning the knife in his hand, the Indian was about to attempt throwing the knife at Jeb, when a shot rang out and the Indian fell.

Jeb came to a kneeling position, breathing heavily when he saw who shot the Indian. Lieutenant Brentwood, crouched with his smoking side arm, smiling. Jeb smiled back. He quickly stood and went to Linda. Grabbing her by the arm, he led her to a safe place and told her not to move. He picked up his Henry and ran back to the large boulder, kneeling by it. Then the Sioux mounted another attack, shouting and shooting as they came, but this time, the troopers beat back the Indians. Not knowing if flaming arrows would start raining down on them again, everyone waited and waited. Nothing. The raid seemed to be over. It looked as if the Indians had had enough. Luckily, no horses were stolen, leaving the lieutenant no other choice but to leave a couple of supply laden wagons behind.

The Army needed those supplies at Camp Nelson, so in order to salvage at least half of the supplies, they would need to load what supplies they could on the other wagons, causing them to be weighted down even further. This action would have caused delays and possibly breakdowns, which Lieutenant Brentwood could not afford. He ordered the wounded taken care of the best they could and the dead be loaded on the wagons.

The Indian attack was disastrous in human deaths and lack of sleep. During their transport of the supply wagons to Camp Nelson, many of the troopers napped, or went to sleep altogether. The one thing Lieutenant Brentwood didn't like was the scalps that Jeb had taken. He was appalled.

When the supply wagons entered Camp Nelson, they were met by the commandant of the post, a Major Mark Ivers. He stood watching the supply wagons roll past him with a joyous expression. Lieutenant Brentwood presented himself to the major. The major asked if he had a good trip and he was immediately told of the attack by the Sioux on the supply wagons at Cedar Creek. The lieutenant also declared he had wounded and dead on those wagons. Then, Major Ivers ordered the wounded be taken to the doctor in the camp, and the dead prepared for burial. Linda Porter was helped down from the wagon she was on by Jeb Winslow, then she and Jeb were also introduced to the major, and she explained why she was at Camp Nelson.

"This is no place for a woman with your upbringing, Miss Porter. No offense meant, but the Wind River

Campaign and Camp Nelson, for the most part, is a very dangerous place, what with Indian raids that could happen anywhere, at any moment." Major Ivers informed her. "And as for Lieutenant Landers, Miss Porter, he should be back anytime. As a matter of fact, he's three days late in returning."

With concern on her face, Linda asked, "should I be alarmed at those three days late, Major?"

"Alarmed is a little extreme. However, I would say concerned is much more appropriate, for the moment."

Linda replied, "thank you, Major, for calming my fears and anxiety a little. My nerves have been on edge ever since Cedar Creek."

"I can only imagine how it was for you, Miss Porter. I'm very sorry you had to go through such an ordeal as Cedar Creek."

Jeb smiled as he spoke up. "She came through Cedar Creek like a trooper, Major."

The major turned to Jeb. "And, you, Mister Winslow. How is it you came to be with the supply wagons, with you being a trapper and fur trader?"

"The Army picked me up, dusted me off, and brought me along to Camp Nelson, Major."

"I see you've been wounded, Mister Winslow. You must see the camp doctor as soon as possible."

Jeb replied, "I'm fit as a fiddle, Major. Linda here, er, uh, I mean, Miss Porter took real good care of me. She's a nurse, ya know."

"No, I didn't."

Jeb said, "one of the best, I'd say."

The major turned to Lieutenant Brentwood. "I expect a full report on my desk by day's end, Lieutenant. The where, what, and how of your trip to Camp Nelson from Fort Bridger."

"Yes, Sir," the lieutenant replied.

The major then said, "but right now, we need to find quarters for Miss Porter."

"Please, Major, call me Linda. I'd feel more comfortable if you did."

"All right, Linda," he replied. He then turned and yelled, "Sergeant Coburn? Escort Miss Porter, I mean Linda to the temporary quarters for the time being."

"Yes, Sir! If you will please follow me, Miss Porter."

Linda asked, "my luggage, Major?"

"I'll have them delivered to you at our earliest convenience."

"Thank you."

Touching the tip of his finger to the brim of his hat, the major replied, "you're welcome."

Then it was just Major Ivers, Lieutenant Brentwood, and Jeb Winslow. Lieutenant Brentwood took a piece of paper from the pocket of his blouse and handed it to the major. "Here is the load sheet per wagon on materials, food supplies, weapons and what type, and of course, the amount of ammunition per wagon and rifle, Major."

The major took the paper and read it, then said, "see that the quartermaster gets this list, Lieutenant. I believe he will find it most useful with unload."

"Yes, Sir. I'll see he gets it." The lieutenant turned to walk away, then turned back. "By the way, Major, the rifle that Mister Winslow is carrying came from the supplies we're bringing. He needed a weapon at the time, and I gave him that rifle and the ammunition to protect himself at Cedar Creek."

Jeb looked at the rifle then said, "I plumb forgot this is the Army's rifle."

The major replied, smiling, "oh, I don't see why he can't have the rifle. Do you, Lieutenant?"

"No, Sir. I don't." He smiled.

Jeb smiled because he got to keep the rifle, then said, "I sure do thank you, and I appreciate it."

The major replied, "well, you did us a favor at Cedar Creek, so as a return favor, you keep the rifle. If you need any more ammunition, see the quartermaster, and I'm sure he will give you all you need."

"If the truth be told, Major," Jeb said, "I was doin' me a favor, too, at Cedar Creek. By not dyin', and I'll surely see the quartermaster for more ammo."

Lieutenant Brentwood said, "and, don't forget to visit the post doctor for that wound."

"You don't suppose?" Jeb started. "No, I reckon not. It'd be too much to ask for, after bein' given this here rifle gun."

"And, what would that be, Mister Winslow?"

"Well, Sir, seein' as how them Sioux done took my ridin' horse and everthing else I owned, traps, furs, and all my possibles, the lieutenant here said I could, most likely, get myself a horse when we got here, but I reckon that'd be askin' too much, huh?"

"Lieutenant, take Mister Winslow to the quartermaster and have him requisitioned a horse, a good horse and ammunition, while I see to the comforts of Linda, uh, Miss Porter."

"Yes, Sir. If you'll follow me, Jeb, we'll get you squared away."

As they walked, Jeb looked at Lieutenant Brentwood and asked, "what does requi-sidual mean, or whatever the major said?"

"Requisitioned? Requisition means you sign a piece of paper and whatever you signed for is given to you, if we got what you want or need."

Jeb looked surprised. "You mean to tell me, all I gotta do is set my mark to a piece of paper and I get what I want from this here quartermaster?"

"That's what I'm saying, Jeb, but you first must have permission from the post commander to do so, in writing."

"Well, if that don't beat all." Jeb paused, then said, "now, wait a minute. The major didn't hand you no written permission paper. I'd-a seen it." The lieutenant showed him the requisition paper from the major he had in his hand and smiled. Jeb shook his head. "I never seen it. That was slicker'n scum off a Louisianer swamp."

"First, we'll get you a horse, saddle and tack," the lieutenant said. "Then ammunition, then off you go to the post doctor for your head wound. And, as soon as your wound is healed, we'll start what you wanted us to do at Cedar Creek."

"And, just what was it I wanted to do at Cedar Creek?" Jeb asked. "I don't recall what that was."

"You don't remember?" asked the lieutenant.

"Uh, uh," Jeb answered. "Refresh my mem'ry."

"You wanted us two to fight for some reason."

Jeb smiled. "Oh, that was plum forgot when you shot that Injun what was tryin' to do me in, Lieutenant. 'Sides, I had no chance a'gin you with my head wound and all. I'd-a lost for sure. Thanks for not takin' me up on it when

I wanted you to. Most folks I know woulda taken the opportunity to do just that, and not miss a lick doin' it, either."

"I wanted to, at the time," the lieutenant replied. "But I knew it wouldn't be a fair fight, so I didn't push the issue."

Jeb said, "just shows how wrong a fella can be about some things, huh? I was wrong about you, sho-nough."

"Well, let's just call it square and be friends. How about that?"

"That suits me fine, Lieutenant," Jeb answered. "Just fine."

With that said, they shook hands and became friends. Before they reached the quartermaster's office, a patrol came into camp. Jeb and the lieutenant turned to see. "That must be Lieutenant Landers and his patrol. Gosh almighty, they look all tuckered out, haggard and torn, Lieutenant. Musta been one hell of a fight," Jeb observed.

"Looks that way, doesn't it?" As he started towards the patrol, the lieutenant said, "since we're friends, call me Jirus."

Walking hurriedly to catch up with the lieutenant, Jeb asked, "do what?"

"You heard me."

Jeb smiled, then said, "yeah, I reckon I did. I just wanted to see if I heard ya right the first time."

As they neared the patrol, Lieutenant Landers had stepped down from the saddle and was greeted by Major Ivers.

Lieutenant Landers turned to a sergeant. "Sergeant Wallace? See to the wounded and walk your horses for thirty minutes."

"Yes, Sir." The sergeant began barking commands.

Then, a man stepped down from his saddle at the opposite side of Lieutenant Landers. Jeb smiled widely as he went to the man and shook his hand vigorously. His eyes sparkled at the sight of this man. "Why, if it ain't Nate Markenson, of all people. I haven't seen you in a coon's age."

"Hello, you ol' horn dog! I'm surprised ya ain't dead and scalped by now," Nate Markenson said, grinning. Then, both said at the same time, "how ya doin'?" They both chuckled at that. As he looked around, Nate asked, "where's Lex and Brent? They hereabouts, are they?"

Jeb's expression went sullen and Nate asked what was wrong. "Both dead, Nate. Sioux ambushed us a while back and took all our beaver pelts, furs and traps, plus the horses and mules. Both Lex and Brent was killed. I was wounded with a war club upside the head. Nearly knocked me outta my socks. They thought I was dead, so they left us without takin' our hair. Why that was, I couldn't venture a guess."

Nate said, "gee, Jeb. I sure am sorry to hear about that. They were nice people. I sure liked 'em a lot. Won't be the same without 'em."

"Yeah," Jeb replied sadly. "I miss not havin' 'em around. But look at you. You look kinda done in yourself. Tough fight, huh?"

Lieutenant Landers answered, "a ten mile running fight. Lost a few good men. Lost some of our horses and supplies. We had to double up, as you can see. The men are just wore out, Major. The Sioux just beat 'em down to a frazzle."

Major Ivers said, "you look about dead on your feet, too, Lieutenant. I'm no doctor, but I'd say a good meal and a good rest will do you some good."

"Yes, Sir. It would."

"But, before you get too comfy, you have a visitor, Lieutenant."

The lieutenant asked, "a visitor, Sir?"

"Yes, Lieutenant. Does the name, Linda Porter mean anything to you?"

"Why, yes, Sir." he replied. "She's my fiancé, Major. She's in Upstate New York. We haven't seen each other in some months. There's nothing wrong, is there?"

"She's here in camp," the major replied.

It's just a marvel how some things can just perk a man up from his weariness and make him forget just how tired he was a second ago. This is what happened to Lieutenant Landers. His face broke out into a wide smile, and he became as jittery as a boy on his first day of school. All nervous like. He was as much surprised as he was happy to know she was here, at Camp Nelson. Joyously, he said, "by your leave, Major." The lieutenant went to walk away.

Major Ivers then said, "just a minute, Lieutenant."

The lieutenant turned again to face Major Ivers. "Yes, Sir."

"I hope her presence here will not disrupt you from your duties. I am quite aware you haven't seen each other in sometime, but proprietaries must be kept at all times, Lieutenant. I'm sure you know there are men here who have families they haven't seen in quite a while as well. Why, I myself, have not seen my wife for nearly a year. I do not wish to see any vulgar displays, Lieutenant. Is that understood?"

"Yes, Sir. Quite understood, Sir."

"You'll find Miss Porter in the temporary quarters next to mine, Lieutenant."

"Yes, Sir," the lieutenant replied. "Thank you, Sir."

Nate chuckled, then said, "if it weren't for you, Major, there woulda been a hullabaloo at their meeting. Might still be one yet, Major. Yes, Sir, might still be one yet."

CHAPTER TWO

Valley of the Warm Winds

As Lieutenant Landers opened the door to Linda's temporary quarters, he just stood in the doorway admiring her. She turned, then smiled, and they both reached out and went to each other. The lieutenant wrapped his arms around her, as she rested her head against his chest, with tears coming to her eyes. The lieutenant raised her head to kiss her, but noticed the tears.

He looked confused and asked, "hey, now. Why the tears?" He released his embrace and held her at arm's length. "Aren't you happy to see me, Linda?"

"Of course I am, silly," Linda answered, as she looked up into his eyes. "I'm just so happy to see you after so many months, it brought me to tears."

He embraced her again. "I'll do my level best for you, Linda. My level best, but right now, our being together cannot disrupt my duties here."

Linda looked confused. "How can my being here disrupt you from your duties?"

Again, he held her at arm's length. "Well, for starters, whenever I go on patrol, you'll be worried for my safety, as well you should, and I'll be worried for you, hopefully not enough to distract me from my duties, but I will be worried none-the-less."

"Major Ivers gave you an order, didn't he?" she asked.

"Yes," he replied. "Yes, he did, and I must follow those orders, no matter how much I want to disobey them."

"I believe he has our best interest in mind."

"That could be. But we are to behave ourselves in front the men who haven't seen their families in quite some time. Even the major hasn't seen his wife in nearly a year. That to me is beyond reasoning, but I'll find that hard to do."

Linda stood back from him, giving him the once over. "Why, just look at you, all dirty, shoddy looking. I think you've ruined your uniform." She smiled.

"I couldn't wait to see you," he said, smiling, "Even in the mess I'm in. It's been a long time since we've seen each other."

Then Linda went to him, and again, buried her head in his chest as he wrapped his arms around her, brushing her hair softly. She softly said, "oh, it's so good to see you again, Paul. It seems an eternity since..."

Then Paul lifted her head and kissed her gently. She seemed to melt in his arms. He released his kiss to look into her eyes. Her eyes sparkled from his tenderness. His eyes were filled with love for her. Then he kissed her again with more force and emotion behind it, hungry for her kiss.

When he finally released his kiss, she looked at him, saying, "my, my, Lieutenant, let me catch my breath." Feigning fainting, she said, "I was expecting something like this, but you still surprised me."

"I best be going. I'm still on duty, you know, and I still have a report to fill out and have it ready for Major Ivers."

"Can't it wait just a little longer, Paul?" she asked.

"I would like it to," Paul replied, "but I don't think the major would like it. We're still under orders about proprietaries."

"No one can see us here," she replied. "I can understand outside, but here?"

"Proprietaries must be kept, Linda. And, if the truth be told, I'm not so sure I can contain my show of love I have for you, no matter where we are. If you need anything, let the major know. I'm sure he can get it for you."

"I need *you*, Paul."

Paul chuckled. "You already have me, Linda. What I mean are material things. Women's stuff we may run short on, if any at all, but anything else, well..."

Linda replied, "I believe I've packed everything I need, Paul, but I may need things later."

"Well," Paul replied, "if you're here for any length of time, maybe we can get the stuff you need at Beaver Falls. It's a town a day's ride from here, but they're not the most equipped place there is. There're women there, of course, but what I hear, they make their own stuff and do not depend too heavily on the general store. Things are hard to come by, what with the Sioux raids."

Linda had a sorrowful look on her face. "I don't believe I'll be here all that long, if you and Major Ivers have your way about it."

"That all depends on Major Ivers," he replied. "And what's best for your safety, Linda. This is no place for you, under the circumstances. This area, twenty miles in either direction, is not safe. The Sioux and the Cheyenne are attacking all over this section. I fear for your safety."

"I know. The supply train I was in was attacked at Cedar Creek. It was the most horrifying, terrifying experience I've ever been in. I thought we were all going to die."

"I was unaware of that. Maybe, when I come off duty, you'll tell me all about it."

"I would prefer not to. I would not like to relive it, even in the telling of it."

"I understand. I'm just thrilled you made it here alive, but I must be getting back to my duties." He tilted his head to one side, then said, "so, I'll see you later?"

"You better or I'll be quite angry with you."

"It's a date," Paul smiled as he replied. "But I got to go for now." He kissed her again, then turned to leave. When he opened the door, he turned to her and said, "see ya. Bye."

"Bye," came the reply.

With that said, Paul closed the door to Linda's temporary quarters, leaving her to stare at a closed door.

****

At a broad board, among many in the makeshift Mess section, Jeb and Nate had just finished eating their lunch when Lieutenant Landers came up to them. They had not risen from their table yet, when the lieutenant said, "Mister Winslow, I hear you were at Cedar Creek when the supply wagons were attacked by the Sioux."

Jeb replied, as he looked at the lieutenant, "I was, and so was Lieutenant Brentwood, Lieutenant."

"I know. I just talked to him and he said you saved Linda, Miss Porter, from being carried away by the Sioux. I wish to thank you for that. I am your servant, in part, as to whatever you want or need. I will do my best to get it for you."

Nate just smiled at Jeb as he turned to look at Nate. He turned back to the lieutenant, then said, "that's awfully kind of you, Lieutenant, but I've already been took care of by the quartermaster. I have what I need for now, but I do appreciate the kind words and intent." He smiled.

"I see. Well, if there is anything I can do, or help you do, you just let me know, and if I can, I will do my utmost in helping you, whenever I can."

Jeb replied, "I appreciate that, Lieutenant, but like I said, I'm already took care of."

Nate then said, "you look all done in, Lieutenant. Sit and have a good meal, then hit the blankets. You look like you could use some sleep."

"Thank you, no," the lieutenant replied. "I'm not all that hungry just yet, but I could use some sack time. Again, Mister Winslow, thank you for what you did for Linda."

"You're welcome, Lieutenant. Just couldn't see her being another squaw for Tah-Tonka-Skah."

Looking bewildered, Lieutenant Landers asked, "who the devil is this Tah-Tonka-Skah?"

"Tah-Tonka-Skah, otherwise known as Two and Two, in American. He has a brother named She-Cha-Chat-Kah, or otherwise known as Tall Man, in American. Both are bad news. Fierce in battle tactics, and mean? He's meaner'n a Timber Wolf when cornered. It was Two and

Two who was leading those red devils what attacked us on the road near the Popo Agie River at the North Fork of the Big Wind River. I recognized him from seeing his ugly face some time ago." Jeb turned to Nate. "It was probably him what gave me this head wound for a keepsake. Whatcha think?"

Nate replied, "I wouldn't put it past him, Jeb. He's as orn'ry as he is cantankerous, and you're right." He chuckled. "He's bad news."

Lieutenant Landers said, "sometime you'll have to tell me why he's called Two and Two, but right now, I'm heading for some sack time, so I'll see you later."

Both Jeb and Nate said in unison, "yeah, see ya," as Lieutenant Landers turned and walked away from the makeshift Mess section.

Nate turned to Jeb as they were leaving the Mess section. "He's a good officer. He's only a lieutenant now, but if he lives long enough, he'll make colonel for sure."

"I have the same feelin' you do 'bout Lieutenant Brentwood. A good officer."

As they walked along, Nate said, "we've seen a few, haven't we, Jeb. Too bad they didn't live long enough to do any good."

Just then, Jeb stopped, causing Nate to stop. "Just what made you become a scout for this man's Army, anyways, Nate? I thought I taught you better'n that."

"Well, I just figured if I was gonna git chased, shot at, and worn down to a frazzle, I might as well git paid for it. Fifty cents a day may not be much, but it ain't nothin' to sneeze at, and still come out ahead, if ya live long enough to collect your pay."

"Trappin' for furs, and baggin' beaver, and huntin' buffaler make a right good livin', don't it?" Jeb asked.

"If ya git to keep it, it does," Nate answered. "But the Sioux and Cheyenne can attack and take whatever you have, includin' your life, but if by chance you do git away and keep your life, you still lose everything you spent months gittin', and come up empty."

"Yeah, I know. I'm where you're talkin' 'bout now."

"Let me guess," Nate said. "You ain't got scratch for a jug, do ya?"

"Not one red penny, Nate. Sioux done took it all. Lock, stock, and barrel."

"Yeah, that's what I figured."

"But, Nate, if you could see yourself clear to..."

Nate chuckled, then said, "I'll take care of ya, Jeb."

Jeb started smacking his lips as if he could already taste the whiskey, then with raised eyebrows, said, "now, ya know darn well if it were the other way..."

"Yeah, I know," Nate replied. "You'd take care of me, huh?"

"Ya darn tootin' I would, that's what friends are for, huh?" Jeb said, joyously.

"Now simmer down before ya bust a gut."

Jeb brought his right knee up and slapped it, saying, "we're gonna have a rip roarin' good time, ain't we, Nate?"

Nate replied, "I only have enough scratch for one jug, Jeb, so with both of us sippin' outta the same jug, may not be as rip roarin' as you'd like."

Jeb said, "well, it beats gittin' jabbed in the eye with a sharp stick, don't it?"

"I reckon it does." He smiled.

Jeb, then scowled. "Only thing is, where is it we find us a jug?"

Nate answered, "that does put a damper on the festivities, don't it? There's no settler store."

Jeb's face brightened, then said, "Quartermaster. If we could talk the major into recki-sidulin' us a jug from the quartermaster, why, then we could have that good time, huh?"

Nate asked, "that's a possible maybe, but I don't know why he would."

"The onliest way to know is go ask," Jeb replied as he smiled.

"Okay, let's just do that, then."

Jeb knocked on the major's office door and they were granted entrance. They walked to the desk as the major asked, "and, what can I do for you two Gentlemen?"

Jeb spoke, "well, Major, Nate and I..." He stopped, looked at Nate, then said, "Go on, Nate, you ask him. I've already got my recki-sidulin'." Nate gave Jeb a hard stare, then Jeb nudged him in the side and said, "well, go on. You ask him."

"Well, Major, we...I mean, I would like a jug of whiskey so's to settle our nerves. I mean, my nerves after such a harrowin' ordeal, if it would please the major."

The major spoke sharply, though trying to stifle a chuckle. "It would not please me, Gentlemen, but it seems it would please you two. Is that it?"

Nate answered, "oh, yes, Sir. It would, Sir, and we'd thank the major kindly, Sir."

"I don't know about you two ruffians with a jug of whiskey. You just might cause an uproar all over camp, what with your rowdy ways, and with a woman on the post."

Jeb then said, "oh, no, Sir. We'll keep it on the quiet side, if you know what I mean, Sir."

"Well, it's against my better judgment, but I believe you two are entitled to have a snort every now and then, to settle your nerves, as it were, so I will grant you your need and desire." Both men stood grinning as the major filled out a requisition slip and handed it to Nate.

Both thanked the major kindly, and as they left his office, he shook his head and chuckled. When they left his office, they were stepping mighty lively. When they handed the quartermaster the requisition slip, the Master Sergeant eyed them real cautiously, but then went to fill the order. When the quartermaster came back with the items ordered, they not only had one jug, they each had a jug. They smiled widely at their good luck, then thanked the quartermaster kindly, and went on their merry way to have their rip roarin' good time. They were slapping each other on the arm and chuckling like two kids in the candy store.

Lieutenant Brentwood couldn't help but notice them acting kind of strange from across the compound. He knew what they had in their hands and chuckled, then with narrowed eyes, he caught up with them and asked, "and, just what is it you two have, there?"

Jeb answered joyously, "a jug of whiskey each, Lieutenant. We're gonna celebrate."

"Celebrate? And, what may I ask are you celebrating?"

Jeb replied, "in two days' time, I survived two Sioux attacks, and Nate here, he came back with Lieutenant Landers' troop alive, under the constant threat of death, I might add, so it's time to celebrate. We're celebratin' life."

Lieutenant Brentwood nodded, "I can't think of no better reason to celebrate, Gentlemen, other than a marriage between a man and a woman, or the birth of a new born."

Nate then said, "then, you'll join us, Lieutenant, in our celebration?"

The lieutenant replied, "I would be all too happy to, only I'm still on duty. But, if you can see it in your means to hold off on your celebration, Gentlemen, then I will gladly join in." Then he spoke in a broken Irish brogue. "But, alas, the hour is late, and the time to celebrate waits for no man." He touched the brim of his hat with his finger. "Good day, Gentlemen." With that said, he walked away with Jeb and Nate staring after him with bewildered expressions on their faces.

Nate turned to Jeb as Jeb turned to him. Then Nate said, "I'm glad I'm a drinkin' man, Jeb, 'cause any more of that kinda talk will surely drive me to drink."

Jeb smiled, then said jokingly, "aye."

Nate quickly looked at Jeb with a raised eyebrow, then said, "oh, hush. You ain't Irish."

As they walked away, Jeb chuckled and said, "I was only funnin' ya, Nate. Honest."

"I know that, ya knucklehead."

"Well, we're fixin' to celebrate, so let us start the festivities!" Jeb said with a grin.

***

Shortly after Jeb and Nate began their celebration in the back of the makeshift corral, a trooper came riding into camp in a real big hurry and headed for the major's office. He was all haggard looking; torn blouse at the lower left arm, ripped to the knee breeches. He reined his horse to a stiff legged halt and jumped from the saddle. It caused quite a stir in the camp, and all came running to see what the trouble was, but before they could get any news, the trooper had already entered headquarters and the major's office. A few minutes later, the major and the trooper came from headquarters. Both had looks of dismay on their faces. As they stood in front of a crowd of troopers, the major went to say something when the trooper fell to the ground.

A few men rushed to help him as the major ordered the trooper to be taken to the hospital. As the same men carried the trooper to the hospital, Major Ivers said, "The Sioux are attacking a wagon train just west of Knotty Pine Ridge, in Lone Pine Valley." He pointed to the trooper being carried away. "Private Harley Walsh was sent to bring us the news. Lieutenant Mason Woods and his troop was in the area and heard the gunfire and went to assist. His troop was nearly cut in half. Those folks are in desperate need of help and I plan on giving them the help they need. Bugler sound Boots and Saddles! I want two troops to ride post haste to their assistance. Captain

Larrabee and Captain Carmichael will lead them. Make haste, Gentlemen! Time's awaistin'!"

The camp was in organized chaos with men running in every direction, getting ready to assist the wagon train under attack by the Sioux west of Knotty Pine Ridge, in Lone Pine Valley. Captain Lance Larrabee was in command of A-Troop, while Captain Ian Carmichael was in command of C-Troop, and both were leaving Camp Nelson in less than twenty minutes.

Jeb and Nate came stumbling from their place of celebration, and in his drunken stupor, Jeb asked, slurring his words, "what in blazes is goin' on here?"

Nate then answered, slurring his words, "I coulda swore I heard Boots and Saddles a minute ago."

Jeb hiccuped, then said, "we must be hearin' things, Nate. Let's continue with our celebratin'."

***

Out in Lone Pine Valley, the Sioux were crisscrossing in a circle around the circled wagons, shouting and shooting as they rode by, inching closer and closer to the wagons, only to be beat back by the men of the wagon train and the Army patrol. It was pure chaos at best. Lieutenant Mason Woods, and what was left of his troop, plus the people of the wagon train were having a time of it, trying to stave off the attack. The noise of gunfire was deafening, and gun powder lingered in the air. The women and children were screaming, afraid of dying.

Lieutenant Woods was shouting orders, but they went unheeded because of the noise. Men, and Indian alike littered the ground around and inside the circle of wagons.

A few women were crying hysterically for their husbands who were killed in the attack. Children ran to and fro, trying to escape the slaughter, unattended because of their dead parents. It was thought it would be just a matter of time before they would run out of bullets against the onslaught of the Sioux. The battle of Lone Pine Valley, had lasted nearly four hours, then a sound that made all the people in the wagon train jump for joy, and yet caused the Sioux to leave the field of battle, shouting and shooting as they left. A bugle sounding Charge!

As the two troops rode hard into the valley, "hip, hip, hooray! Hip, hip, hooray!" came from the people of the wagons. People were standing and cheering as the troopers chased the Sioux from the field.

Standing amidst the rubble was Lieutenant Woods, with a smoking sidearm in his hand, smiling just as wide as he could smile, and what was left of his troop. He looked around himself at the destruction and the deaths the Sioux had wrought upon these people, and those of their own. As Captain Larrabee and Captain Carmichael dismounted just outside the circle of wagons, Lieutenant Woods stepped over some breastworks to meet them. He saluted the captains. "I see Private Walsh made it to

Camp Nelson! And am I ever glad to see you! Just didn't know how much longer we could hold on here. Refill on bullets was getting hard to come by."

Captain Larrabee and Captain Carmichael stood and surveyed the destruction, and the people who lay dead and wounded, including those of the Sioux. Then, Captain Carmichael said, "we came as soon as we got the word, Lieutenant. Glad to see you made it."

"So am I, Captain. So am I." He paused, then said, "I was afraid Private Walsh didn't make it. I saw a few of the Sioux braves chasing him, and I saw his horse go down, but that was all I saw. I got busy elsewhere, as you can imagine."

Captain Larrabee replied, "lost a lot of good men today. May they never be forgotten."

The children were finally caught up by a few of the women and curtailed from their running, though both woman and child were sobbing almost hysterically.

Captain Larrabee yelled to a trooper who was sitting his horse nearby. "Bugler? Sound recall." The bugle sounded Recall and soon a thunder of horses' hooves was heard as the troopers came back to the area. Both captains and Lieutenant Woods were greatly surprised when the troopers brought back a captive Sioux brave, being held up between two horses by the arms.

A trooper then reported, "this chucker wood's horse was wounded in the frey, Captain, and just run itself to death, then toppled this Indian as we came upon him. Stupid. Pur-dee, downright stupid, thinkin' he could outrun a horse. Just took off runnin', he did."

Just then there was a rifle shot and the Indian tumbled backwards from the impact of the bullet. Their heads turned to a woman, standing in the circle of wagons, with a smoking rifle in her hands. She then dropped the rifle, sobbing incessantly, with her hands to her face. Every man who was near the Sioux brave, breathed deeply and sighed a heavy sigh. It was an even bet each man thought, *what if she'd missed?* They turned to look at the body of the Sioux brave with a bloody hole in his chest.

Back at Camp Nelson, Jeb and Nate came from their place of celebration, shouting and hollering loud enough to raise the dead. They raised quite a commotion as they near staggered across the compound. Most of the troopers laughed at their condition. They held onto each other as if the one held the other up as they walked, er, uh, staggered. The major heard the commotion from his office and went outside to see what was going on. He then saw what the commotion was all about and shook his head as he chuckled. "I knew it was against my better judgment to let them have a jug of whiskey." He then yelled to a sergeant, who was standing near him, "Sergeant Harris? Put those two under arrest for being drunk and disorderly and have them sleep it off in the stockade."

"Yes, Sir." Sergeant Harris turned and yelled to a couple of troopers who were walking by, "you two, help me put those two yahoos in the cooler."

One of the troopers answered, "okay, Sarge."

As the sergeant and the two troopers walked up to Jeb and Nate, the sergeant said, "by order of Major Ivers, you two are under arrest for being drunk and disorderly. You are to sleep it off in the hoosegow, so let's go."

Jeb replied, in his drunken stupor, "say what?"

The sergeant answered, "you heard me. Let's go."

Nate, also slurring his words, replied, "I think he said we're under arrest..." He turned to the sergeant and asked, "what was it again, Sergeant?"

"Drunk and disorderly."

Nate turned to Jeb. "Drunk and disordersly, Jeb."

Jeb asked, "how do ya like bein' arrested for... what was it, again, Nate?"

"Drunk and disordersly, Jeb."

"Do you like bein' arrested, Nate?"

Nate scowled, saying, "I don't care for it at all, Jeb. Not one iota."

The sergeant then said, "we're here by order of Major Ivers to put you two in the hoosegow, so let's go, you two."

Jeb turned to the sergeant. "Just you three?"

The sergeant replied, "we'll get it done."

Jeb scoffed, "oh, yeah? You and whose army?"

"Are you two resisting arrest?"

Nate replied, "in a word, yes." At that said, he laid a haymaker upside the head of one of the troopers.

The trooper's head turned with the punch and his eyes rolled back into his head as he slowly slumped to the ground with a dreamlike look on his face. Then, the fight ensued. Jeb and Nate were having the best time of it. Jeb, at one point, picked the sergeant up from the ground, who had been knocked down by Nate. Jeb brushed him off gingerly, then asked, "you alright, Sergeant?"

As he stood on wobbly legs, the sergeant replied, "a little dizzy, is all."

Jeb looked at the sergeant with concern, then asked, "you sure you're alright, Sergeant?"

"As soon as I shake the cobwebs," the sergeant replied. Jeb chuckled as he waylaid the sergeant again, causing him to tumble backwards onto the ground.

Jeb and Nate were holding their own, until other troopers joined in on the tussle. Then they began to lose ground. They were eventually held by two or three troopers each, and then they were escorted to the stockade, cursing every few steps.

When the doors to their cells were closed and locked, Jeb shouted, "it took all you blue bellies to get the job done, you rats!"

Nate joined in on the insult, yelling through the bars, "rats! That's what they are. Rats!"

The sergeant in charge of the stockade yelled, "oh, shut up, you drunken hooligans."

Pressing his face against the bars, Jeb shouted, "I ain't no hooligan, you peckerwood. I'm a republican, you no account...." Then, his voice faded into mumbled words.

"Well, here we are, Jeb," Nate said as he stood and stared at the bars to his cell. "Never thought I'd ever be in here, for sure."

Jeb replied, "of all the nerve of that no account sergeant..."

Nate interrupted, saying, "they were just following orders, Jeb. It was Major Ivers who ordered us thrown in the hoosegow."

"We weren't disordersly, were we, Nate?"

Nate was moving his jaw back and forth to check if it was out of place, or something, then replied, "depends on what you call disordersly, Jeb. The major musta thought so, or we wouldn't be in here."

"I reckon so, but when we get outta here, I'm gonna give the major a piece of my mind. Ya hear that, do ya?"

"I hear ya," Nate answered. "But you'll be back in here with more time to spend."

Jeb chuckled, then said, "it could be you're right." He laid down on the clapboard bed in his cell. "When I do give him a piece of my mind, I'll end it with Sir."

"It's best you don't say anything a-tall, Jeb. Think what ya want, but don't say it."

"Why shouldn't I say it? He put our celebration on the short stick, plus I don't answer to him, if ya git my drift."

Nate turned to Jeb. "Well, seein' as how you're at Camp Nelson, and he is the man in charge, you do answer to him. Plus, he gave you a horse and rifle you didn't have because of what the Sioux took from you. At least you owe him that much." He stretched out on the clapboard bed in his cell, then said, "he didn't have to give you anything. Remember that."

"Yeah, well. You sure know how to see the silver linin' in ever cloud, don't ya, Nate?"

"Oh, hush, Jeb. I'm tired and sore from my soberness, and I just wanna git some sleep, so hush."

Disregarding what Nate had told him, Jeb said, "I sure do miss Lex and Brent. Wish they was here. Well, not here exactly... oh, ya know what I mean."

"I know what ya mean, Jeb. I sorta miss 'em, too, but you knew 'em better'n I did."

"They'd sure help a fella out what was in a pinch. Never knew two nicer fellas, 'cept you, of course." Then, from Nate's cell, he heard snoring, so he smiled widely, pulled his weathered hat down over his eyes, and was soon asleep himself. His dreams were disconcerting at best. He dreamed of Lex, Brent, and himself, riding the high lonesome, where the Eagle flies. Then it switched to them riding after buffalo in their giant herds. He also found them trapping beaver along the outlying tributaries of the Big Wind River, constantly on the lookout for the Sioux. It seemed he tossed and turned all night long. His sleep was quite unrestful. How he longed to have his friends back at his side. Then, he dreamed of the day it happened, when the Sioux killed his friends, and took all they had worked for for so many months.

He became very angry and started to thrash around on his clapboard bed, so much so, it woke Nate up from his sleep. He stirred, and finally came to his feet, then went to the bars that separated them and began to yell at Jeb to wake him up and stop his thrashing around.

Jeb groggily woke up. "What? What is it, Nate?"

Nate answered, "you woke me up with all that thrashing around and mumblin' to yourself. What's got into you anyways? Can't a body git some sleep around here?"

Jeb raised himself and threw his legs over the edge of the bed. "I'm sorry, Nate. I guess I was dreamin'."

"I reckon so. You was dreamin' so hard and loud, it woke me up."

"What time is it?" Jeb asked as he stretched and yawned, sitting on his clapboard bed.

Nate yawned, then said, "pert near daylight." As he stretched himself, he said, "Just a couple hours, or so, I think."

All was quiet in the stockade, except for Nate and Jeb. Breakfast was in the making. The aroma of it came through the windowed bars that allowed fresh air into their cells.

"You smell coffee, Nate? I sure do."

"Yeah, I do," Nate replied. "And, just smell them biscuits, too. I hope they have sausage gravy with 'em. Taste mighty fine right about now. My stomach is beginnin' to think my throat's cut."

Jeb asked, "wonder if they'll let us out in time for breakfast?"

"One can only hope. Least ways, I hope they do."

"It'd be a rotten shame if we was to eat our breakfast in here. This is a raggedy smelly old place. Stinks to high heaven in here."

Nate replied, "ya sure that ain't just your upper lip blowin' back in your face?"

Jeb turned to Nate, then said, "oh, ha, ha, ha. Ain't you the funny one this mornin'?"

"If you think bein' in here is funny, you're crazy."

Jeb answered, "I was talkin' 'bout you, you nit wit."

***

Out in the Wind River Valley, what the Indians call Valley of the Warm Winds, a woman screamed hysterically. It echoed a short way, then faded against the majestic waterfall, which was cascading down into the Big Wind River. Rich green grass, and an array of beautiful multi-colored, full leaf trees that simply took your breath away. Amidst this background, the Sioux had jumped a homesteader in the Valley of the Warm Winds. They had killed and scalped a woman's husband and made her watch. She screamed maniacally, as she was being held by two Sioux braves, scoffing at her, and her dead husband. There were no children. The two were just starting out, building their dream, and make a life of their own. Believing the woman had completely lost her mind, the Sioux released her, for it was against their religion to harm a person who they thought their mind was gone. Before leaving, they burned the cabin.

A few days later, trappers came through the area and found the remains of the man and that of the woman. From the look of things, the woman had taken her own life. As for the man, they knew what happened. They saw the near-built log cabin that had been burned, and the trees that were felled, leaving tree stumps sticking out of the ground. Before the trappers left, they buried both man and woman, leaving no grave markers, but mounds of fresh dug earth that would disappear with time.

The trappers had no earthly idea who these people were or how long they had been in the Valley of the Warm Winds. The cabin had been burned and all identification of who they were or where they come from, vanished in the flames. When the trappers reached Beaver Falls, they informed the authorities what they had found and where they found it. It is not known whether or not the deaths of the man and woman were ever investigated by the county authorities, but the fresh dug earth was covering an all too soon forgotten memory. The trappers traded beaver pelts, furs, sold what they could. They stayed three days to hoot and holler, and have themselves a real good time, with a jug in one hand, and a soiled dove in the other.

Then, on the fourth day, they resupplied themselves, and headed out, traveling towards the Valley of the Warm Winds. The tributaries off the Big Wind River supplied beaver, muskrat, martens, and river otters, and on occasion, wolf skins. Bear skin was worth its weight in gold.

Many of the easterners loved a bear skin rug in front of the fireplace, and these trappers, among others, were more than happy to oblige. The only problem was the Sioux, with their almost ever constant habit of showing up when you least expected them. More than a few times, they showed up, leaving the trappers no other recourse but to save their lives and leave in a hurry, but a few had not been so lucky and lay dead where they fell.

Jeb and Nate were released from the stockade and had enjoyed their breakfast in the Mess section as if nothing had happened. Lieutenant Landers enjoyed a restful night and woke feeling refreshed and ready for duty. Major Ivers had eaten his breakfast in his office, knowing he had decisions to make this day. He was yet to hear from Captains Larrabee and Carmichael as to the condition of the wagon train attacked by the Sioux, nor about Lieutenant Woods' troop availability to Camp Nelson. Miss Linda Porter had left her luggage partially unopened, not knowing if she would be leaving sooner than she thought, but she did change her attire for the day. She also decided on having her breakfast in her temporary quarters, not wishing to cause the men more anxiety of not having their loved ones with them.

It was near mid-day before Captains Larrabee and Carmichael with their troops, and the remnants of Lieutenant Woods' troop came into camp. It caused quite a stir among the troopers in Camp Nelson. Major Ivers met them and waited to hear what had happened, and the condition of everyone involved in the attack.

Captain Carmichael turned in his saddle, saying, "Lieutenant Ames, dismiss the troop, then walk your horses for thirty minutes."

"Yes, Sir."

Captain Larrabee turned to Lieutenant Woods. "Lieutenant, you will be needed in the major's office to give a detailed account of your actions when you engaged the Sioux as they attacked the wagon train."

"Yes, Sir."

Then, the three officers dismounted and met Major Ivers at the entrance to headquarters. They rendered their salutes and the major returned. He shook hands with each officer, then said, "I'm glad to see you made it back alive, Gentlemen, instead of being draped over your saddle, as I see many are."

The three responded in unison, "thank you, Sir."

Major Ivers then said, "Sergeant Harris, take the wounded to the hospital and prepare the dead for burial."

"Yes, Sir."

Major Ivers turned back to his officers and said, "shall we go into my office? I most assuredly want to hear every detail of what happened."

Lieutenant Woods asked, "what of Private Walsh, Major?"

"He's doing just fine, now, Lieutenant. Just fine."

Lieutenant Woods said, "I would like to award him with the Medal of Valor, if I could, Sir."

"I knew you would, Lieutenant, so it is already in his service jacket. I have no such medals on the post at this time, but I will order quite a few from Fort Bridger for such men as Private Walsh for their bravery."

Lieutenant Woods smiled. "Thank you, Sir."

"Oh, by the way, Gentlemen, I have taken the liberty, and the honor, to post in your service jackets as well, the Medal of Valor for each of you for this action."

"Thank you, Sir."

The major chuckled, then said, "I have the feeling I will be handing those out as if they were cake at a Sunday get-together. The brave men and officers of Camp Nelson deserve them."

With a sweeping motion of his arm, the major said, "after you, Gentlemen."

Lieutenant Woods replied, smiling, "no, Sir. You first, as always, Major."

Major Ivers smiled. "As you wish, Lieutenant."

Captains Larrabee, and Carmichael said, in unison, "you first always, Major."

Major Ivers replied, "very well, Gentlemen. If you will follow me." With that said, they went into headquarters to make an account of troop actions when they engaged the Sioux in the attack on the wagon train.

CHAPTER THREE

The Thick of Things

At that moment, Linda Porter and Lieutenant Landers were having a private discussion on her length of stay at Camp Nelson in her temporary quarters. Linda had seen the battered, bruised, wounded men of Lieutenant Woods' troop as they entered Camp Nelson. Even though she herself had been in an Indian attack at Cedar Creek, she worried about the health and safety of her beloved, Lieutenant Paul Landers.

She asked, "just how much longer will it be until I am told I must leave Camp Nelson for my safety, Paul?"

"I don't know, Linda. I haven't talked to the major today, and as you have seen, he's rather busy with his official duties. Lieutenant Woods' patrol took quite a beating when they went up against the Sioux."

"But, surely, he must realize I'm in more danger on the stage," Linda argued, "but well-fortified here at Camp Nelson."

Paul turned from her, walked a few paces away, then turned back to her. "It isn't my call, Linda, but I'm sure the major took that into account. If you were to leave on the stage, he just might give you an escort..."

"Escort!" rebuffed Linda. "You know as well as I do, the Sioux are liable to attack in large numbers against the patrol." Paul stood staring at her as she turned her back to him. "And, when the escort leaves the stage?" She turned back to him. "Then what?"

Paul went to say something, but stammering in his answer, he finally replied, "I don't know, Linda, but your being here has put me in kind of a tight spot. Not wanting to disobey orders, but worried for your safety, here or on the stage." She stood staring at Paul. "Myself and the major have stated, fifty miles in any direction is not safe, not with the Sioux killing anything white."

Linda abruptly turned from him, saying, "then, you and Major Ivers agree that I must leave Camp Nelson, and soon."

"I don't want you to leave, Linda," Paul retorted. "I was quite happy to hear you were here, but as I and the major have said, it is not safe here for a woman of your ... your stature. We're living by our own wits here, Linda. This is a rough and tough life, but it's the life I have chosen, so..."

Linda turned back to him and questioned, "and, you don't think I'm strong enough for this kind of life? I'm not strong enough? Is that it, Paul?"

Paul reluctantly replied, "well, no. It's just that things are different than it was in New York."

"Then, that is exactly what you're saying, isn't it? You don't think I can be a military wife, living a life, where from one day to the next, may well be the last day

I see you alive, and not draped over your saddle as they bring you in. Or, maybe you will be buried in some nowhere, forgotten place, unknown marker, murdered by the Sioux or the Cheyenne."

"Linda?"

In her anger, Linda announced, loudly, "Hush up! I'm talking, and I'm mad."

Paul just smiled, saying, "yes, Ma'am."

Linda continued angrily, "I've traveled over 1500 miles to be with you, and all you can do is conspire with Major Ivers on how to get rid of me. I don't understand that, Paul. I've suffered hardship after hardship. Why, I was even attacked by the Sioux, and when I do get here, you want to send me away. Why is that?"

"Actually, it was over 1700 miles, and it's for your own safety, Linda."

"Don't correct me!" Linda retorted. "My safety? How can you say that, Paul, knowing full well, no matter where I am, I'm in danger of attack, according to you and Major Ivers?"

"That does present a problem."

"A problem? Now, I'm a problem, Paul?"

"Nothing that can't be resolved, Linda."

"Yeah, I know," she replied, as she turned from him. "By sending me away."

Paul went to her and placed his hands on her arms. "If you'll just listen to reason, Linda."

"Reason?" she asked softly. "What reason do I have left?"

"Linda, be reasonable."

Linda turned quickly to Paul, then said, "the only reason I'm here is because I love you, and want to be with you, no matter the danger. Is that so hard to understand?"

"I understand completely, Linda, but..." At that second, the bugler sounded Boots and Saddles. Both Paul and Linda turned toward the sound of the bugle. With urgency in his voice, Paul said, "I need to go, Linda. I may be needed. We'll talk about this later."

As he headed for the door, she uttered, "Paul?"

At the door, he turned and smiled, then said, "we'll talk later. Okay?"

"Okay," came the reply.

Paul opened the door, then closed it behind him, leaving Linda to stare at a closed door. As anxiety and concern took hold of her, she again screamed, "Paul?"

A second, or two later, Linda rushed from the room, quickly following Paul, stopping just shy of the compound, and watched Paul enter headquarters. As she stood there, she watched as the troopers of Camp Nelson prepared for trouble, somewhere. From her vantage point, she witnessed the major, Paul, and a few officers come rushing from headquarters.

The major was barking orders and the officers and men hurriedly obeyed those orders. The officers were barking orders, as the non-coms were barking commands. Each man saddled his horse, then mounted. In a steady flow of horses, they assembled, and were waiting in line, per company, per troop, ready to go, somewhere. Where, she didn't know. Amidst the organized chaos of Camp Nelson, she tried to find Paul, but among the assembled troopers, she could not. Her eyes showed the desperation she felt as she searched feverishly for him. When she finally did locate him, she waved frantically at him. Sitting astride his horse beside Paul was Jeb Winslow as scout for the troop.

Jeb noticed Linda waving in their direction, so he waved back. Paul turned to Jeb with narrowed eyes and said, "she's waving at me, Winslow."

Jeb replied, "it's hard to tell with us sittin' aside each other, Lieutenant."

"If ever we're beside each other from now on, and Linda waves in our direction, be it known, Winslow, she is waving at me. Is that understood?"

Surprised, Jeb replied, "touchy, touchy, ain't we, Lieutenant?"

"I am. With her being here, she's put me in a rather precarious position."

Jeb replied, "ya mean between duty, and her safety, huh?"

Paul answered, "that's about the size of it."

Jeb chuckled, "Good luck with that, Lieutenant. Women do the strangest thing when it comes to love."

Paul gave Jeb a quick look, lowered his eyes, slightly shook his head, then said, "I know."

Looking around, Jeb asked, "reckon how many we are, Lieutenant?"

"At east two full companies, Winslow. Hopefully it will be enough. Our numbers have grown since we've been here to arm the settlers against Indian attacks and try to put a stop to the attacks altogether, if that's possible."

Jeb replied, "tryin' to prove both peoples can live aside each other in peace, huh?"

"As I said, Winslow, if that's possible."

Jeb replied, "that's a noble cause, Lieutenant, but I highly doubt it."

The lieutenant gave Jeb a quick look, and went to say something, but then Nate shouted at Jeb from two rows over. "Hey, Jeb! I thought I taught you better'n that. Becomin' a scout for the Army."

He laughed uproariously, as Jeb replied, "oh, ha, ha, ha."

Just then, the major mounted his horse, went to the front of the companies assembled, raised his hand and shouted, "Company! Forward! Ho!" dropping his hand in a forward motion.

As the two companies left Camp Nelson, Linda stood staring after them. She wondered, *will this be the last I see Paul alive?* She went back to her temporary quarters and went to the open window that looked out onto the compound and watched as the last of the troopers left Camp Nelson. When she could no longer see them, she lowered her head to rest on her chest, and just above a murmur, she said, "Paul?"

***

As the column rode steadily in their line of march, two abreast, the major turned in his saddle and yelled from the front, "First Sergeant Finnley, scouts and outriders if you please."

"Yes, Sir." Then, with just a wave of his hand, scouts and outriders left the column. After their leaving, the column closed ranks to fill the empty places. The column wound back and forth like a snake on the trail, as the trail rose and fell, and wound around with the terrain. The only noise was metal against metal, horses' footfalls, a man would cough or sneeze because of the dust being raised. Men chatted back and forth quietly in different areas of the column on a myriad of subjects.

After a few hours, the major called a halt to the column. Turning in his saddle, he announced, "pass the word, prepare to dismount!" The word was passed and the troopers anticipated the next command. Then he announced, "pass the word, dismount!" The word was passed, and as if watching dominoes, the troopers dismounted down the line. "Pass the word, walk your mounts!" The word was passed as each trooper anticipated the next command. "At a walk, forward!"

As the column moved forward at a walk, there was chatter among the troopers for a bit, then it slowly died down to no more chatter. After a thirty-minute walk, the major announced, "Company! Halt!" As the column halted, he announced, "pass the word, mount."

The word was passed and as if in reverse dominoes, the troopers mounted their horses. He then announced, "Company! Forward! Ho!" There was no need to relay that command. The troopers at the head of the column moved out, reining their horses to a walk. All that was needed for those back down the line to do, was just follow the crowd. Again, the only sound was the sound of many hooves, and the sound of metal on metal.

As the column wound its way like a snake over small hills, gullies, and creeks, Jeb Winslow, being a scout, came racing back to the company. Major Ivers raised his hand, commanding the column to halt, as Jeb short-reined his horse to a halt just a few feet in front of Major Ivers. "What is it, Winslow? Trouble?"

"Could be, Major. I crested over a hill about three miles from here to a meadow that stretched far and wide, when..."

Major Ivers, interrupted, "get to the point, man. Indians?"

"Yes, Sir. A whole passel of 'em, just t'other side of Johnson's Creek. Tepees everywhere."

Major Ivers then asked, "do you know how many, if you were to guess? Are they Sioux?"

"Some are, Major. Miniconjou to be exact. Mostly Arapaho, though. Some Fox. To my way of thinkin', there must be at least 1500 or better in there. As I said, Major, a whole passel of 'em."

Major Ivers replied, "yes, you did say that, didn't you." He sighed heavily, then asked, "did you happen to find a route around those Indians? I don't want to invite trouble. I would prefer to avoid it, if possible."

"I did. If we was to stay to the foothills, there's a chance they might not hear or see us, but with this crowd, I don't see how that will be possible. Plus, they'll have mounted sentries and outriders looking for any sign of trouble, so they're sure to spot us soon enough."

"I see your point, Winslow," he replied. "It seems we're too many to not be heard, and yet, not enough to take them head on, doesn't it?"

Jeb rubbed the back of his neck, then replied, "I don't know, Major. That all depends on your way of thinkin'."

"Well, Winslow, my way of thinking is, we stay to the foothills, and take our chances, being as quiet as we can. Muffle our horses' shoes if need be. It could work."

"Anything to keep them red devils off our backs, Major. That just might do it, but these metal rings on these saddles can be heard from quite a ways away."

"I'll take your advisement under consideration, Winslow."

Jeb replied, "you best, Major, or they'll be all over us thicker'n flies at a church social. But it's your show. If you choose not to, well then, I'll see ya, Major. I like to choose my own time and manner in which to die, and this one ain't it."

Major Ivers sighed heavily, then said, "point taken, Winslow. We'll do as you suggest." He turned in his saddle, then said, "pass the word. Muffle your horses' hooves with whatever you have handy and silence those rings."

The word was passed down. It took a while, but then, after a while, they were ready.

Jeb then stated, "it's best we walk our mounts part way, Major, then when we get just shy of 'em on the other side, we can mount horses again, in order to skedaddle."

"I'll follow your lead on this, Winslow, but you better be right. I want to avoid a fight if possible."

The column moved out at a walk, leading their horses by the reins. Each man was scouring the countryside for possible signs of danger. It took a little over an hour to pass the encampment without being heard or seen, which pleased Major Ivers.

Then, the order was given to unfetter their horses' hooves and rings. When this had been done, the major ordered, "pass the word, prepare to mount. Mount."

The word was passed, and when each man had mounted, he ordered, "Company! Forward! Ho!"

When the company had traveled about ten miles, they came upon a small rise in the terrain and the major called a halt. He sat looking at the Big Windy Way Station, or what was left of it. Most of it lay in rubble and burning timbers. He turned in his saddle. "Captains Larrabee and Carmichael, and a troop each, follow me. You, too, Winslow."

Captains Larrabee and Carmichael called out their prospective troop, and with scout Jeb Winslow, followed Major Ivers to the station at a fast gallop. At the way station, Captain Larrabee and his troop went to one side, while Captain Carmichael went to the other side, encircling the station as Major Ivers dismounted and walked among the ruins. Jeb had dismounted and walked with Major Ivers. They found the stage in shambles and a burning hulk.

Tied to one of the wheels of the stage was the ghastly remains of a man, or so it was assumed, burnt beyond recognition. There were three more bodies around the station, two men and a woman, all three in their early to mid-thirties, if one was to guess.

The men had been scalped and the woman had been stripped naked, then staked out on the ground, spread eagled. She had an arrow protruding from her left breast, and the bottoms of her feet had been stripped of layers of skin. She lay with her eyes open, staring into nothing with her face in a frozen expression of a horrible death. Finding a blanket lying nearby, Jeb knelt, closed her eyes, then covered her body with the blanket. The corral fencing had been torn down and set on fire. The six draft horses and one riding horse had been put to death, lying in a stench about the corral. The barn and the station had been torched and had fallen in on themselves. The stench from the dead horses and the burned body was so foul, the troopers had to cover their noses with their neckerchiefs.

Graves were dug, while the effects of the dead were gone through, what they could find, to find out who these people were. Jeb recognized the station manager, the stage driver, but the rest, he didn't. There were no papers or letters to tell who these people were. The man who was burned at the wheel was unrecognizable, even to his own mother. Being unable to find out who these people were didn't sit too well with Major Ivers, but the reason was understood. "Arapaho, Winslow?"

"Naw," Jeb answered. "Cheyenne, Major." Grabbing an arrow and inspecting it, he then said, "Cheyenne dog soldiers to be exact, according to the etchings on this arrow."

"Cheyenne?" Major Ivers asked, surprised. "Well, that puts a twist in the tail, doesn't it?"

Jeb replied somberly, "it would seem so, Major."

Major Ivers took the arrow from Jeb, looked at it, then said, "who'll show up next? The Sioux?"

"Could be," Jeb answered, shrugging his shoulders. "They may come snoopin' around to see what happened here, if they're anywhere's nearby, they will, then we have those behind us."

Major Ivers said, "Arapaho."

Jeb just nodded his head yes.

Major Ivers threw the arrow away from him. "Well, we best be moving, then."

The major turned to go to his horse. "Is everything to your satisfaction, Captains?"

Both Captains Larrabee and Carmichael replied, "Yes, Sir."

"Good," Major Ivers replied. "Then, let's be on our way, Gentlemen. We may be having Sioux company, if they're not already here, watching." As he mounted his horse, and the two troops were back among the column, he commanded, "Company! Forward! Ho!"

As the column moved out and the last trooper left the area, two Sioux braves on horseback came from their hiding places and watched in what direction the column was going. Then, they headed back to where the main group of Sioux were encamped to tell what they had seen.

The column followed the trail that skirted the Big Wind River for a few miles, then the trail meandered away from it as the river made a hard left turn in a southerly direction. Each man was aware an Indian attack was eminent. They followed the trail that led away from the river, up a small hill into more densely populated tree-covered hillside. It was unavoidable to keep the noise down from the fallen, dried, dead leaves and brush that had accumulated on the trail. Song birds in the trees stopped their singing as they approached.

As the column went up one hill, then down and up another, it wound its way around on the trail like a crawling snake. Jeb and Nate were scouting a mile or two ahead of the column. Indian scouts were out farther than they were, about half a mile. Nate stopped and dismounted, searching the ground for recent tracks of unshod ponies. There were many. He turned to Jeb.

"Whoever these tracks belong to, there's a-plenty of 'em."

Jeb asked, "how recent do ya think, Nate?"

"Not more'n a couple hours at most," Nate replied, turning in the direction of travel, pointing in that direction. He then said, "same direction we're goin'."

Jeb said, "ya don't suppose..."

Then, gunfire erupted from the direction Nate had pointed, and it caused a knee jerk reaction from both men. The sound of gunfire didn't travel very far amongst the trees and hills at a high-pitched sound, but it did travel far enough for Jeb and Nate to hear the noise. Nate hurriedly mounted his horse, and he and Jeb took their rifles from their scabbards and took off in a hurry. They had traveled no more than half a mile when they came upon what looked like eight or nine Indians firing at one lone Indian. The lone Indian was making a good show of himself against the many. He was the Crow scout, Arapoosh, meaning Sour Stomach. Jeb and Nate were very much impressed with Arapoosh, so much so, they were chuckling as they entered the battle. Holding the reins in their teeth, they raised their rifles and fired. Two Indians fell.

Surprised by the two white men charging at them, guns blazing, the Indians broke and went running from the field of battle, screaming their war cries as they left. Jeb and Nate found Arapoosh had a bullet wound to the left leg just below the knee. In his broken English, he had said the Ute Indians had surprised him and he got his leg wound. Jeb and Nate both replied that they had seen them. While Nate chased down Arapoosh's pony, Jeb stood guard in case the Ute decided to have another go at them. It took a few minutes for Nate to find and wrangle Arapoosh's pony, but when he had, he led the pony back to where Jeb and Arapoosh waited.

Jeb had torn a piece of cotton from his own leggings and tied it tightly around the leg wound. They were soon joined by the Pawnee scout, Kuruk, meaning Bear, who sat his pony watching. Arapoosh hobbled over to his pony, and with the help of Nate, mounted. He moaned and grimaced a little from the pain. Kuruk just smiled, then turned his pony, riding from them in the direction he had just come.

Nate said, "you take Arapoosh back to the major, Jeb, while I follow Kuruk in case he's ambushed by the Ute. If they can surprise one Indian, they can surprise another."

"Well, you best be careful, Nate," Jeb replied. "I've already lost two good friends. I don't want to lose you, too."

Nate smiled. "You worry too much."

"With good reason, I should think," Jeb answered. "You mind what I tell ya, ya hear."

Nate replied, "would you git outta here before Arapoosh bleeds to death. Now, go on, git!"

"Alright, already. I'm goin', I'm goin'."

Before Jeb reined his horse away, Nate slapped him on the leg. "You best be careful, yourself. The Utes may still be around, settin' up another ambush."

"Now, who's worrin', huh?" Jeb smiled.

"I reckon we're both worry warts. Now, go on, git!"

As Jeb and Arapoosh reined their horses away from Nate, he yelled, "you mind what I say, Nate. Ya hear me? Hang on, Arapoosh."

Then, away they went, back to the major at a full gallop. Nate just shook his head as he went to his horse and mounted, then reined in the same direction Kuruk had taken. The Arapaho, the Sioux, the Fox, the Cheyenne, and now the Ute. A body began to feel all boxed in with nowhere to run. Surrounded is more apropos for this turn of events. It began to seem as if all knowing eyes were watching every move. Without seeing another Indian, the hair stood up all over the body. Anxiety showed its ugly head, with a whole lot of nervousness to go around.

It only took a second or a missed planned ambush, for your whole world to be turned upside down, and the possibility of you seeing through empty eyes with an Indian haircut. It has that distasteful flavor that would ruin your whole outlook on life, or lack thereof. Within ten minutes or so, at a fast run, Jeb and Arapoosh reined their horses to a stiff-legged stop in front of the major. The major had already halted the column upon seeing Jeb and the Crow scout returning. It was clearly seen that the wound from Arapoosh's leg was bleeding badly, leaving blood splatters on the pony's belly. Jeb dismounted, then helped Arapoosh from his pony to sit on the ground. Arapoosh was rubbing his leg, grimacing from the pain.

The major asked, "what happened, Winslow?"

"Utes, Major," Jeb answered. "Arapoosh fought them off bravely, but received that leg wound, then me and Nate helped a little, and we chased 'em off."

Surprised, the major replied, "Utes? I thought they had moved out to Montana. Just how bad is that wound?"

"Not nary as bad as it looks, Major," Jeb replied. "Bullet went clean through. No bone broken, but he'll be sore a few days, if'n it don't git infected. He'll hobble some, I reckon."

"Find yourself some clean bandages to stop that bleeding, Winslow." He then shouted, "Sergeant Harris, help Winslow with that man's wound. A field dressing will do."

"Yes, Sir." Sergeant Harris dismounted, and with a medical pouch, attended to Arapoosh's leg wound.

While this was going on, the major himself dismounted and stood watching. "Just where did this happen, Winslow? We heard no gunfire. None whatsoever."

"A couple miles or so up the trail, Major. Me and Nate was close enough to hear the noise, so we hightailed it up there and we found the Utes had Arapoosh pinned down, so we chased 'em off. There were eight or nine, Major. We killed two. Arapoosh killed three."

"What of the Pawnee scout? What's his name?"

Jeb replied, "Kuruk, Major. Yeah, we seen him. He came riding in just after the Ute ran away, the jackals. Kuruk went back to scouting, I reckon. Nate followed just in case he was ambushed."

Then Arapoosh sucked in a healthy breath of air as Sergeant Harris wrapped his leg with the field bandage. Sergeant Harris said apologetically, "Easy now. Sorry. I may have wrapped it too tight."

Arapoosh released his breath of air erratically, then said, "too tight."

"I'll loosen the bandage."

In his broken English, Arapoosh replied, grimacing, "thank you, Ser'gent."

The major said, "well, Winslow, it seems we're closed in. Utes ahead of us. Arapaho and Fox behind us. God only knows where the Sioux and Cheyenne are. It would seem we have no choice but to continue on, and hope we avoid a fight of huge proportions."

"And, just where are we goin', Major?"

"If you must know, Winslow,' he replied, "the Copper Penny Mining District. It's a mining community where they mine for copper, three miles this side of Garden City."

Jeb said, "that's still a fer piece to go, Major. Ten mile or better. Ever been there?"

"No, but I've heard of it. From the request I received from the now territorial governor, John A. Campbell, they've been harassed by the Sioux and Cheyenne. The miners have requested our assistance in thwarting those attacks. A few men have already been killed in the last month or so, with countless horses and mules taken. *That's* where we're going."

"That's a tall order, Major."

"That's what we've been assigned to do, and we'll get it done, or die trying."

Jeb chuckled. "I don't mind the tryin', Major. It's the dyin', I mind."

The major turned to Sergeant Harris. "Are you done yet, Sergeant?"

"Yes, Sir. Just finishing up, Major."

Major Ivers then asked Arapoosh, "you able to ride, uh, Aristotle?"

Arapoosh looked at Jeb, then turned back to the major, and replied, "have to. Name, Arapoosh."

Jeb chuckled a little. "That answered that question, eh, Major?"

The major gave Arapoosh a dead pan look, then said, "well, get him on his horse. We're leaving."

Jeb went to assist Arapoosh to his horse, when the major said, "don't you have scouting to do, Winslow? We'll take care of him."

"Alright, Major. I git your drift."

Major Ivers turned to Captains Larrabee and Carmichael. "Send out your scouts, Captains. We are in need of their services."

"Yes, Sir."

He then turned to Arapoosh. "You're to stay with the column for now. Try to avoid hard riding until that wound heals, if possible."

Arapoosh gave a nod of his head. Sergeant Harris helped him upon his pony. Arapoosh grimaced and let out a low moan at sitting his pony.

Major Ivers then said, "hurry up any chance you can, Sergeant. We haven't got all day."

"Yes, Sir." Within a matter of a couple minutes, Major Ivers and Sergeant Harris had re-mounted.

The major then raised his hand and commanded, "Company! Forward! Ho!" dropping his hand in a forward motion. The column moved out, slow at first, then they rode at a canter. The trail wound its way up and down and around the hillside, making it look like a moving snake. The sound of many hooves and the ring from the brass rings on the saddles and head gear on the horses were the only sounds heard.

Out a couple miles from the column, Jeb was retracing his tracks from where Arapoosh was ambushed by the Ute, and where he left Nate. About a half mile past the area, and a hundred yards ahead of him, a covey of quail took flight from a densely covered area, scattering. He knew he had not caused that flight of frenzy, so he carefully approached that area knowing it could be an ambush in waiting. The area where the quail had taken flight was just off the trail, easily accessible to where he was riding. His instincts and a gut feeling told him to be wary, so he stopped his horse, pulled his Henry from the boot, levered a round in the chamber, then he rode slowly towards it. When he came abreast of the area, he kicked his horse in the ribs, and from the jump, the horse was running at a full gallop.

Then came the warbled war cries from the Indians waiting in ambush, curling the hair on Jeb's body. Gunfire erupted as the Indians started shooting at him. The Sioux had come from hiding to give chase. He kept turning in the saddle, looking back to judge the distance between him and the Sioux, which wasn't far enough for him. As the bullets whizzed passed him, he crouched over the saddle to make himself less of a target. He only hoped they would not shoot his horse out from under him, tossing him to the ground. Up and over, around about, the chase went as Jeb tried desperately to elude his attackers. He would cradle his rifle in the crook of his arm and fire at his attackers, but he would miss often.

If you've never heard the warbling sound of the Sioux war cry, it is fierce, awesome, and terrifying at the same time. Makes a man's blood run cold at the sound of it. The heart beats faster, nerves tingle all over your body, the hair on the body stands up like trees. Fear is instant in the mind, causing some men to be rattled, losing his wits, not knowing what to do. Some men shake all over, then faint dead away, thus never to wake up. Jeb was not that kind of man, to faint dead away. He had a score to settle, but this was not the time nor the place for revenge. Self-preservation was his utmost thought. Not having his hair lifted was another, for sometimes, they gave you an Indian haircut while you were still alive, just because they could.

The trail led Jeb and the pursuing Sioux, into a densely forested area. With the Sioux hot on his trail, Jeb went up a small incline in the trail, then down the other side, where a short time later, when the Sioux arrived, they were fired upon from the thickest part of the trees. Sioux braves were falling from their ponies by bullets ripping into them, causing them to falter in their attack. They finally ran from the area at a high rate of speed, shouting and shooting as they left.

Jeb reined his horse to a stiff-legged stop, then turned his horse to see what had happened. From out of hiding, Nate came from one side of the trail, while Kuruk came from the other side, both holding Henry rifles. They rode to where Jeb sat his horse waiting for them. When they arrived, Nate was chuckling. Kuruk just smiled a wide, toothy grin.

Nate said, "I can bet they were surprised!"

Jeb pushed his hat farther back onto his head. "I know I was. Where'd you two come from, anyways?"

"You have Kuruk here to thank for that little ambush. It was his idea."

Kuruk said. "Uh, me go." He turned his pony and rode away down the trail in the direction Jeb was heading.

Jeb said, "Ooo-wee. That was a sight for sore eyes. You, and now Kuruk, are my best friends. Thanks for savin' my hide, not to mention my hair, from a Sioux yard stick."

At the mention of friend, Nate's expression turned somber and he rested his hands on the saddle horn. "Speaking of friends, Jeb..." he cleared his throat, then said, "I found Willoughby."

With raised eyebrows and a smile, Jeb said, "you did? How's he doin'? Why it's been near..." Then it dawned on him with the word *found*. His eyes narrowed as he asked, "what do ya mean, you *found* Willoughby?"

"I found him staked out, face down, over a fire pit. He was a mess."

Confused, Jeb asked, "well, how do ya know it was Willoughby, Nate? You know as well as I do, a fire pit will make a man unrecognizable by his own mother."

"Trust me," Nate said. "It was him."

Jeb asked again, raising his voice an octave, "but how do ya *know*?"

"His tattoo. Ya know the one on his shoulder that says Mother? You can't burn somethin' like that off completely. Some of it was still there. It was him."

Jeb looked bewildered and lost. "Did you...?"

"Yeah. I put rocks over him. Said good words over him, too. I couldn't dilly-dally too long, though. I did the best I could, under the circumstances."

"Well, that's good you did that at least. It hardly seems possible, Nate," Jeb said. "That's a total stunner and an ill pill to swallow." He shook his head slightly, then said, "he was a good friend and he will be sorely missed."

"I'll miss his humor most of all. That man would laugh harder at his own jokes than you would." Nate chuckled, then said, "sometimes, he just tickled his own self." His eyes began to glisten over a little as he said, "Ignatius Willoughby was quite a man."

"Where was it you found him?" Jeb asked.

"Just this side of Hawthorn Creek. Quiet place. Near Flushing Meadows. Beautiful scenery there. He has a great view of the creek where he's at."

"I've been through there." Jeb sighed heavily, then asked, "well, you ready?"

"If you are." They reined their horses to the trail and got back in the thick of things.

***

When the column had eventually reached the area where Arapoosh had been ambushed, eight or nine Sioux braves blocked the trail, mocking them, laughing at them, taunting them to give chase. They then turned and rode away quickly, screaming the Sioux warbled war cry. Surprised by this bold move on their part, the major called a halt to the column and quickly recalled many a fool's errand at such a tactic as this. To give chase would only amount to an ambush. The officers, and men took a personal affront to the Sioux's actions and somewhat demanded the major chase them down and give them a complete thrashing for their actions.

Major Ivers turned his horse to face the column. "As you were, Gentlemen. We will not give chase. An ambush has been planned and if we do give chase, we will fall into their trap."

Captain Larrabee replied, "but Major, there are only eight or nine of them."

"Leading to how many, Captain? Two, three hundred, or more? I will not chase a hare down a rabbit hole into a den of vipers."

Captain Larrabee gave a staunch reply, "No, Sir!"

"Trust my words, Captain," Major Ivers said. "Unless I miss my guess, before this day is through, you will have your fill of Indians. If we survive the day, Sir."

Captain Larrabee replied, "yes, Sir. Your orders, Major."

"Carbines at the ready. Locked and loaded, men. Pass it along." The word was passed, and every man followed those orders. "Captains Larrabee, and Carmichael, have your best marksmen cover our rear guard."

"Yes, Sir."

As the men broke ranks and went to the rear, Major Ivers, then yelled, "Lieutenant Rutherford, front and center, if you please."

"Yes, Sir." The lieutenant broke ranks and went to the front of the column. "Yes, Sir?"

"Have your best marksmen to the rear to cover our rear guard as well."

"Yes, Sir."

As Lieutenant Rutherford rode back to his troop, Major Ivers said, "let's prepare to move out."

As soon as they were ready, Major Ivers raised his hand, "Company! Forward! Ho!" He dropped his hand in a forward motion and the column moved out. Every man, with their weapons locked and loaded, were ready for what they knew was coming their way. Indians. Which ones would be anybody's guess. The Sioux? Ute? Cheyenne maybe? The column finally left the foothills and found themselves advancing on Hawthorne Creek, near Flushing Meadows.

There, they found a mound of rocks, presumably a burial mound, done by someone in a hurry. It was distinguished by a handmade, wooden cross stuck between the rocks at the head of the mound at a slight angle, looking as if, at any moment, the cross would fall over. As the column passed the mound, every eye was on that mound, wondering who was in it and did they know him? More befitting for the moment, how did he die and when? Each man was alone in their own thoughts as they began to have thoughts of their own mortality, which now, seemed questionable. As they rode past the mound, all was quiet among the ranks. Some troopers had the look of somberness to their faces, while others had looks of despair.

As they crossed Hawthorne Creek, the water splashing brought the troopers back to reality, but not to the point of erasing the thought of their own mortality. All a man could do, was the best he could, and not worry about what he could not change, nor disregard as fate. *If the fates allow*, was an ever present saying among the men of Camp Nelson. It was a sign of great respect and character in a man, not only by how he lived, but how he died. There is such a thing to a man as *he died well*. His memory will never perish, and his name will be brought up many times, in the passing of time. His name will be written down in the annuls of military history, or remembered over campfires, told to the young, so his name and his deeds, will not be forgotten.

CHAPTER FOUR

The Rescue

As the column got closer to the Copper Penny Mining District, the more the Sioux harassed the rear of the column with small bands of warriors to have the troopers give chase, and away from the Copper Penny Mining District. Within a mile, or so from their intended goal, the troopers heard gunfire. The major knew the Copper Penny was again under attack, and so the reason for the small harassment at the rear guard of the column. Major Ivers ordered the deployment of two troops, one to one side of the attacking Sioux, led by Captain Larrabee, and the other troop, led by Captain Carmichael, to the other side, while he took the main column into the middle of the attack, splitting the Sioux attackers in half. This maneuver would, at least, stifle the attack and thus render a stop to that attack.

Major Ivers ordered the bugler to sound the charge. At the sound of charge, he said, "well, Gentlemen, leave us go amongst them." And the company joined in the fray at a full gallop. The action was ordered chaos and intense. The Sioux attackers splintered as the troopers from each side cut them down and drove them from the Copper Mining District. The ground was littered with dead and dying Sioux. Out of the sixteen men at the Copper Penny, five men had been killed, but no horses or mules were stolen. Seven troopers lost their lives in this action against the Sioux. Gun smoke hung in the air, and the surviving men at the Copper Mining District stood and cheered the troopers as the Sioux withdrew from the attack.

A casualty list had been made and handed to Major Ivers. After reading it, he had a glum look on his face. He looked at Captain Carmichael with narrowed eyes, then asked, "are you sure of this, Captain?"

"I'm sorry, Sir," Captain Carmichael replied. "But yes, Sir. I'm sure." He gestured with his right hand. "He's over here, Sir."

They walked over to where Captain Larrabee lay with an arrow through his neck, paralyzing him from the neck down, but fully awake, for the moment. He tried to talk when the major knelt beside him, but he could not.

Major Ivers said, "it's no use to try and talk, Captain, for you cannot. You have been paralyzed, probably from your neck down, so your vocal chords will do you no good."

Captain Larrabee looked up at him with fear in his eyes. Major Ivers put his hand on the captain's arm. "I'm sorry, my friend, but there is nothing I can do to help you. If you're in pain, blink your eyes once for no and twice for yes." Captain Larrabee blinked his eyes once, yet the fear remained in them. Before Major Ivers could say anything else, the light went out in Captain Larrabee's eyes.

He reached down and closed the captain's eyes. "It was just a matter of time, Captain. I am so sorry. Rest in peace, Sir." As he rose to his feet, he said, "Captain Carmichael, form a burial detail and bury these men, but before you bury this man, please remove that arrow."

"Yes, Sir. I'm sorry, Sir."

"Thank you, Captain. Such are the hazards and risks of a soldier in the time of war."

Captain Carmichael replied solemnly, "yes, Sir. It is."

A burial detail had been formed for the troopers who were being buried at the same time the miners were putting the dead on wagons, carts, and whatever afforded transportation to Garden City for the family members to have a proper funeral with family and friends to mourn over the loss of life of a loved one. After the burial of the troopers had been completely, the major ordered a ten-gun salute for the dead. Five men were chosen, and they stood side by side at the grave site. Captain Carmichael was charged with that salute.

The men stood in attendance for the burial and the salute. At the ready, Captain Carmichael gave the command, "Fire!" The five men raised their rifles and fired, then reloaded their weapons. At the ready, he again gave the command, "Fire!" The five men again raised their rifles and fired. They then reloaded their weapons.

As Major Ivers turned to walk away, Captain Carmichael again gave the command, "Fire!" The five men again raised their rifles and fired.

Major Ivers looked confused at the last salute and asked, "why the fifteen-gun salute, Captain?"

"The men requested that for Captain Larrabee, Sir. I was obligated to make that request happen, Sir."

"You did so without consulting me, Sir?" Major Ivers asked.

"Yes, Sir," came the reply. "The men wanted to surprise you, Major. They knew how fond you were of Captain Larrabee, and they are as well, Sir. He was a fine man, and a good officer."

Major Ivers surveyed the men in his company with pride. "Yes, Captain. Men. He was a fine man, and a damn good officer. Thank you, Gentlemen. Thank you."

Then the whole company replied loudly, "you're welcome, Major."

Major Ivers was taken aback by that resounding welcome. His eyes began to glisten so he turned from the company as he was overcome with emotions.

Captain Carmichael turned to the company and commanded, "Company. Dismissed."

Regaining control of his emotions, Major Ivers then turned, "be ready to move out, Captain. We're leaving in fifteen minutes."

"Yes, Sir." Captain Carmichael, then turned to the company barking orders to prepare for leaving. As the major was talking to the surviving men of the Copper Mining District, the troopers were preparing to leave. Pleasantries were exchanged between the men of the mining district and thanks were given for the stoppage of the Sioux attack.

Major Ivers commanded a full troop to remain and protect the miners from attacks. He also outfitted the miners with guns and ammo with superior fire power against attacks.

The troop to remain was commanded by Lieutenant Rutherford. As the troop left the column, Major Ivers noticed each man standing by his horse ready to leave. "Pass the word, prepare to mount." The command was passed, and each man put his foot in the stirrup, and grabbed the saddle horn. "Pass the word. Mount." The word was passed, then each man mounted his horse.

Major Ivers looked back over his shoulder at the company behind him, raised his hand in the air, then commanded, "Company! Forward! Ho!" dropping his hand in a forward motion. As the company moved out slowly, Major Ivers reined his horse to the right, going in the direction from which they came, and the column followed in a pivot right wheel. It was just about then that Jeb and Nate joined the column. Major Ivers gave them a questioning glare. Both men stared back with raised eyebrows.

"And, where the devil have you two been? Out lollygagging elsewhere, I suppose, instead of here with us, breaking up an Indian attack against those miners."

Nate replied, "well, Major, we had troubles of our own. We couldn't be here to help you because we were pinned down by a small party of those red devils."

Jeb spoke up. "When the main attack was broke up by you, they took off lickety split. It took a few minutes to catch up our horses."

The major replied, "well, at least you showed up. Glad you two made it."

Nate replied, "we're kinda glad for that ourselves, Major."

"What of the Pawnee scout? What's his name?"

Jeb replied, "Kuruk, Major, and he's dead. He came to our defense, and they cut him down."

"I'm sorry to hear that. He was a good scout."

Jeb asked, "what about the Crow scout, Arapoosh, Major?"

Major Ivers replied, "we'll know that when we get to where he is, Winslow. His condition would not afford him being with the company during this action. I had him remain behind with his wound."

Nate then said, "well, hopefully he's still alive. Small bands of Sioux are all over this area."

"I hope you're right, Markenson," Major Ivers replied. "I left two troopers with him."

Jeb said, "Nate and me, we'll just ride on ahead, Major, to make sure, alive or dead."

The major replied, "we're headed that way, Winslow, but you two go right ahead. I need to know what's out in front of us anyway."

Both men replied, "right, Major." Then both men slapped leather to their horses and were soon out of sight of the column.

Major Ivers turned in his saddle and commanded, "Captain, we need two men who are good at scouting and guides immediately."

Captain Carmichael replied, "Yes, Sir."

Major Ivers then commanded, "Sergeant Finnley, outriders if you please."

"Yes, Sir."

Sergeant Finnley waved his hand and the outriders left the column. The column rode at a steady pace back toward Camp Nelson. When they had come to the place where Major Ivers had left the Crow scout, Arapoosh, and the two troopers, expecting to see them, he found only Jeb and Nate waiting for them. Major Ivers gave the command for the column to halt. He looked around, then placed his hands on the saddle horn and asked, "and just what are you two doing? Where's the troopers I left, and the Crow scout?"

Jeb answered, "the troopers are dead, Major. Where Arapoosh is, we don't know."

Nate then said, "I have a gut feeling the Sioux took him to make an example of him."

The major asked, "an example? To whom?"

Nate replied, "oh, to the next settlers camp, or the next town, wherever the white man can be found. They will torture Arapoosh at a safe distance from any gunfire, but the people will surely see, and hear him scream, before he dies."

Major Ivers then said, "that is a distasteful image I do not care to see, Gentlemen. Have these *people* no shred of decency."

Jeb and Nate just shrugged their shoulders, then Jeb said, "it depends on the meaning of the word decency, Major, but it does send the message loud and clear, no matter how inhumane we think it is. You see, Major, these Indians don't believe the same way we do, nor do they think the way we do, so take that for what it's worth."

"But, you yourself have said you'd extract vengeance against those Indians who killed your friends. Did you not?"

"I did," Jeb answered. "Oh, I didn't say I liked these Indians, Major, or any Indian. I hate 'em for what they did. I only explained the difference between them and us. They will soon git their comeuppance, in due time. Trust what I say, Major. Trust what I say." He turned to Nate and asked, "you ready?"

Nate replied, "as I'll ever be."

"Let's go, then."

As Jeb and Nate reined their horses away from the column, Major Ivers asked, "and just where do you two think you're going?"

They reined their horses sideways on the trail, then Nate responded, "where else? To find Arapoosh and git him back. Alive, if possible."

The major yelled, "I need you here!"

Jeb yelled back, "he needs us more, Major."

With that said, they reined their horses away from the column again, and at a high rate of speed, left Major Ivers shouting, "but, how do you know which bunch... has...him?"

Captain Carmichael reined his horse up next to the major and asked, "shall we go after them, Major, and arrest them on the charge for dereliction of duty, Sir?"

Major Ivers sighed heavily. "No, let them go, Captain. They're on a mission of mercy, if you want to call it that."

"More like desertion, if you ask me, Sir."

Major Ivers looked at Captain Carmichael. "Their desertion, as you put it, Sir, is in defense of a friend, to remove him from danger, or... to make sure he doesn't face it alone." He breathed in heavily, then breathed out slowly. "I only hope they make it in time."

Captain Carmichael's face showed the regret of having said what he said. "Yes, Sir. So do I."

"You were only thinking of Army regulations, Captain, but Army regulations have no meaning with those two, so let's have no more talk of it."

"No, Sir. Thank you, Sir."

***

Just a few miles from where they had been, Jeb and Nate halted their horses. They were searching the ground for tracks as to which way the Sioux, who had taken Arapoosh, had gone. They knew Arapoosh's pony had a slight defect on the right front hoof and was rather hard to find, what with all the tracks from the Sioux unshod ponies going anywhere and everywhere. Finally, after much searching, they found the hoof defect. They followed the track to make sure of the direction it was going, then they knew. To the northwest, towards Beaver Falls. They also knew the Sioux had to stop somewhere to send out scouts to find out if the Army was there, or at least in the area.

The Sioux did not want a confrontation with the Army, and a needless battle to ensue before or during the torture of their captive Crow enemy. Jeb and Nate rode at a full gallop towards Buffalo Falls. Then, within a few miles of town, the Sioux made an abrupt left turn, adjacent to Beaver Falls towards the Popo Agie River. Jeb and Nate followed slowly, not knowing when they might stop to send out their scouts, and to discuss their form of torture, and prepare for that torture. It may take a while before the scouts returned to make their report. In the meantime, they had already decided what form of torture for the Crow enemy that would send their message loud and clear to the white man who lived in wooden tepees.

Jeb and Nate finally dismounted. Moving as quietly as they could through the trees, they came close to the Sioux encampment. They noticed the Sioux had staged their ponies away from camp. The only pony in camp was Arapoosh's pony. He was sitting his pony with his hands tied behind his back with a semi-straight piece of wood to keep him erect while being tortured. Jeb and Nate knew they had to find their pony herd and run them off, and then somehow rescue Arapoosh from certain death. They moved quietly and assuredly to find the pony herd. It took a few minutes, but they finally located the herd. They knew it would be guarded, and it was, by two braves.

Knowing they had to do away with those braves, they decided to come from both sides of the pony herd. They separated and when they had come to their point of attack, they pounced on the Sioux braves. Using only their knives as they came up from behind them, they covered their mouths with their hands and thrust the knives into them, thus eliminating their warnings to those in the camp. Shaking off their deed, they waved their arms in the air and began shouting to scatter the ponies. Smiling at their success, they ran toward the camp, avoiding the onslaught of Sioux trying to recover their ponies. When they reached the camp, there were still two braves in camp. One brave held the reins to Arapoosh's pony.

The pony began to dance, causing the brave to try and control him. When he turned to do so, that's when Jeb jumped him from ambush. The other brave turned to fire his weapon but suddenly received a stabbing blow with a knife to the heart. The brave sank slowly to the ground to die in the dirt. Jeb grabbed the reins to Arapoosh's pony and quickly led him away from the Sioux camp. They rushed to their own horses, leaving Arapoosh the way they found him until they were safely away from the Sioux.

When they considered themselves safe, Arapoosh shouted, "cut me loose!" Nate took his knife and cut the bonds that held him. When he did, the piece of wood fell to the ground. Arapoosh slid from his pony, stretched himself, and rubbed his wrists where they had been lashed together, as he hobbled around.

Nate asked, "are you okay, besides the leg wound?"

In his broken English, Arapoosh replied, "yes. Arapoosh okay." Jeb twitched his neck and winked at Arapoosh. He was taken aback by that, then said, "me not *that* okay." As Jeb chuckled, he said, "not laughing matter, Jeeb." He sat his pony rigidly and straight-faced as Jeb and Nate mounted their horses. When they had mounted, Arapoosh said, "we go! Quickly."

"That's good advice," Jeb replied. Then all three men kicked their horses in the ribs and quickly left the area.

They headed back to where they believed the major and the column should be, or thereabout. When they got to that location, no Major Ivers or the column. Nate asked, "did we miss 'em?"

Jeb replied, "with that crowd? Naw. Either we're late, or they are."

Arapoosh asked, "what now, Jeeb?"

Jeb answered, "well, for right now, we look at that leg wound. Your pony has blood spatters on his belly, and that means that wound has opened up again."

Arapoosh replied, "better wounded, than not care if wounded."

Nate said, "meanin' dead. I hear ya, Arapoosh."

"Me glad. Not wish to say again, Nute."

Jeb started chuckling, then said, "Nute. Now, ain't that the funniest thing?"

Nate replied, "Oh, hush up, Jeeb." At that said, both men were chuckling.

As he sat his pony, Arapoosh shook his head, and with raised eyebrows, he said, "you fellows, not funny." Which caused Jeb and Nate to laugh heartily.

Jeb then said, "climb down, and we'll take a look at that wound."

Arapoosh slid from his pony, then sat down on the ground, favoring that leg. As Jeb removed some of his bloodied clothing from his lower leg, Arapoosh moaned. Jeb noticed the bandage had come loose, allowing the blood to run and splatter. He uttered to Nate, "looks bad, Nate."

Nate scrunched up his face. "How bad?"

Jeb turned to look at Nate. "Hot iron to stop the bleeding."

"That bad, huh?"

"'Fraid so. You git a fire goin' and..."

Nate interrupted, "now? We need to find Major Ivers, or have you forgotten that?"

Jeb replied harshly, "no, I ain't forgot that. He needs it done, and done now, Nate."

"Well, of all the dumb luck. We do this, he'll be out for a day or two, and we can't afford that loss of time."

"Better than him dyin' from loss of blood. Ask him. Go on, ask him."

Confused, Nate asked, "ask him what?"

"If he's c o l d," he spelled out. "If he is, then it's hot iron, now."

Arapoosh asked, "what is c o l d, Nute?"

"It means cold, Arapoosh." Nate acted like he was shivering by grabbing his arms, and shaking back and forth, saying, brrr. "Cold. Are you cold?"

"Little," came the reply.

Jeb then said, "what'd I tell ya. Build a fire, Nate."

Nate started to argue. "Now, hold on, now. Let's see if that's what he wants to do. After all, he's the one who'll be taking the hot iron."

"Well, then ask him, and find out what *he* wants to do."

Nate asked Arapoosh, "do you...?

Jeb nonchalantly said, "I hope he does the right thing."

Nate looked at Jeb, but said nothing. Turning back to Arapoosh, he again asked, "do you...?

Jeb said, "it's against my better judgment, if'n he don't."

Nate turned back to Jeb. "Would you just hush, so's I can ask him?"

Jeb turned his head in a huff. "Just sayin'."

Nate sighed heavily, then said, "you are incorrigible, my friend. Won't let a feller ask a simple question for a question what needs asked." He turned to Arapoosh once more and said, "we need to stop the bleeding, Arapoosh, if not, you may bleed to death, or worse, gangrene may set in, and you'll lose that leg. No matter what, we need to cauterize the wound and stop the bleeding."

Arapoosh looked at Nate, then Jeb, then back to Nate. "The Popo Agie River not too far. Couple miles, maybe. Take me there, then use hot iron, stop bleeding."

"That's not a bad idea, Jeb. We can cauterize the wound, then use cool water to cool it down."

Jeb asked, "think you can make it?"

Arapoosh looked at Jeb and answered, "have to."

"Yeah, I reckon ya do, huh?"

As Nate helped Arapoosh on his pony, he said, "I just hope we don't run into a Sioux war party. They're everywhere, it seems." After the three had mounted, they took off for the Popo Agie River.

When they were about a half mile from the river, Arapoosh fell from his pony. The pony ran a few yards, stopped, turned back, and snorted. Jeb and Nate reined their horses to a stiff-legged stop, then turned and went back to Arapoosh.

Nate said loudly, "he's passed out."

"I see that." As they were dismounting, Jeb said, sarcastically. "I just hope he didn't break his dang fool neck."

They picked Arapoosh up and threw him over his pony, belly down. Jeb took a rope and quickly tied his hands together, tossed the rope under the pony's belly to Nate, who tied the rope around his feet to keep him from falling off again.

They mounted hurriedly and took off towards the Popo Agie River, with Jeb leading Arapoosh's pony behind him by the reins. At one point they stopped among a stand of trees that awarded some concealment from a small war party of Cheyenne braves lurking in the area, searching for someone or a group of white men to wage war against. When they had passed without notice, Jeb and Nate hightailed it to the river. Finding a densely treed area that could afford some protection from being seen, and where smoke from a small fire would dissipate into the trees, they dismounted and carefully removed Arapoosh from his pony. They laid him down on the ground and removed the bandage Jeb had put on his wound.

They built a small fire and placed a knife in the coals to cauterize the wound. Jeb said, "we may have to gag

Arapoosh from screamin' out when we cauterize that wound. His screamin' will bring in unwanted company."

Nate replied, "good idea." Looking around him, he then said, "he'll most likely pass out from the pain and stay out for a day or two. This looks like a good place to stay 'til he's ready to ride again."

Jeb removed the knife from the coals of the fire, then said, "not quite yet," then put the knife back in the coals.

The lapping of the water from the river up against the bank and the sound of rushing water was soothing to the ear, but they knew they could be spotted at any time, no matter how well they were concealed. They both stood guard as the knife became hotter and hotter.

Jeb removed the knife again and it glowed flame red, then he said, "it's time, Nate."

"Let's git him gagged." Nate raised Arapoosh's head and put a piece of cloth in his mouth, then tied a piece of cloth around his mouth to stifle his scream.

Jeb said, "hold his leg while I apply the hot iron. Don't want him floppin' around either."

Nate grabbed his foot, pulled it straight, then said, "okay."

Jeb applied the hot iron to Arapoosh's wound and he screamed as he came to a sitting position. He tried to grab his leg from the pain, but could not. His eyes were still closed. Jeb armed him back to the ground and he passed out again. The cloth gags had worked. Arapoosh screamed into the gags and it went just so far, then died out. Jeb and Nate grabbed their weapons and waited to see if they had been detected. Surprisingly, they had not been.

They waited a few minutes, then Nate took a rag and reached into the river for cool water, then squeezed the cool water onto the wound. He did this for a few minutes as Jeb crouched on one knee guarding against any unfriendly guests.

They doused the fire and settled back for a long stay on the Popo Agie River.

Jeb reached over and placed his hand, palm down, on Arapoosh's forehead, and said, "he's burnin' up with fever, Nate."

Nate, then wet the rag again and wiped Arapoosh's forehead and face with it. He did this a couple of times, then left the cool rag on his forehead. "Now, we wait." He wet the rag on regular intervals and wiped Arapoosh's face with it on a regular basis as Jeb kept guard.

Between cool water on his wound, face, and forehead, they ate from their pouch of jerked meat and crackers. A cold camp was in order. A time or two, they heard horses' hooves close to them, but they had not been spotted. Yet.

Just above a whisper, Nate asked, "wonder where Major Ivers is?"

Jeb answered, "I been wonderin' the same thing." Then, silence fell between them.

The trio stayed by the Popo Agie River for a day and a half, standing guard over their patient, as it were, guarding against any unfriendly guests, and waiting for Arapoosh to stir awake. Then, mid-day on the second day, Arapoosh stirred and came awake. As he lay there, he asked, "where?"

Jeb turned to him, whispering, "Shh. Popo Agie River. How you feelin'?"

Arapoosh replied, in a whisper, "groggy. You use hot iron?"

Jeb whispered, "yeah."

"How long, be here?"

Nate whispered, "a day and a half. We'll leave in the mornin'."

"Good. Not feel like riding. Better tomorrow. Why whisper?"

Jeb whispered, "Cheyenne and Sioux war parties in the area. Be real quiet."

"Thank you, friends."

Jeb tapped Arapoosh on the arm, then whispered, "you're welcome, my friend."

Arapoosh closed his eyes and went back to sleep. Jeb and Nate smiled at his coming awake so soon. Then they heard a twig snap not far from them. They bellied down with their weapons ready. It was a few minutes of nervous sweat 'til they saw a figure coming through the trees. A man on foot, crouching, coming at them. Then they saw it was no Indian. A white man dressed in mountain man fashion. Who is he? How did he know they were here? Does he *know* they're here? What does he want? These and other thoughts were going through their minds.

As the man neared them, he stopped, waiting. What was he waiting for? He looked around through the trees, then kept coming. When he got within twenty yards, he knelt, and just above a whisper, he said, "Winslow?" He paused, then, "Markenson?"

Jeb, and Nate looked at each other. Then Jeb said, "I know that voice." Coming to one knee, he said, "Tobias? Tobias Canfield? Is that you?"

Tobias then said, "show yourselves."

Nate asked, "are you Tobias Canfield?"

"Yeah. It's me. Tobias Canfield. So, show yourselves."

Nate came to a kneeling position. "Over here. Come ahead on."

Tobias Canfield finally came to where Jeb and Nate were waiting for him. He took a knee and said, "I found ya. Took a while, but I found ya."

Nate asked, "and why is it you're lookin' for us?"

"Major Ivers sent me to look for ya. Said you'd gone to fetch a Crow Indian scout from the Sioux. He wanted me to find out if you're alive or dead."

Jeb said, "well, as you can see, we're very much alive."

Tobias noticed Arapoosh lying near the river's edge and asked, "that him?"

Jeb replied, "yeah. That's him. Cauterized his leg wound day before yesterday. We'll be leavin' come mornin'."

"Mornin', huh?" Tobias asked. "Not a good idea, Jeb."

"Oh?"

"Uh, uh," he said. "Big pow-wow. Big medicine. Large gathering of the tribes in this area. We need to move and be quick about it. They'll be thicker'n fleas on a hound dog soon enough" He looked over at Arapoosh, then asked, "he able to ride?"

Just then, Arapoosh raised up, resting on his elbow. "Have to. Heard talk. Tie me to pony, if must."

"Smart Injun. Let's move, quickly. Get him ready while I fetch my horse." Then Tobias crouched and moved away from them while Jeb and Nate gathered their horses, then helped Arapoosh on his pony. Arapoosh moaned at that.

Nate said, "can't be helped, my friend."

"Arapoosh know."

Jeb then asked, "you think you can make it without being tied down?"

"Not know." He grimaced from the pain, then said, "Tie anyway." Quickly, they tied Arapoosh to his pony, mounted, then rode toward Tobias, who was mounted and sat waiting for them.

Tobias said, "hurry every chance ya can. It's gonna get very busy with unfriendlies, and soon." As they met up with him, he said, "let's git."

They kneed their horses and quickly made it for Camp Nelson, hoping they wouldn't meet a party of Indians in their quest. They soon found themselves where the Arapaho village used to be. They had moved. Where? Unknown.

They were near Johnson's Creek, when a small band of Cheyenne noticed them. They gave chase, shouting and shooting, with their warbled war cries causing the skin to crawl and the hair to stand up all over the body. All four leaned over in the saddle to keep from being such a big target. As the four raced along the road with the Cheyenne hard on their trail, they exited the densely populated tree line that led to the trail that skirted the Big Wind River. They took that trail in a hurry toward Camp Nelson. They were soon overtaken by a cavalry troop who was on patrol and heard the commotion, thus saving the four men from death or injury at the hands of the Cheyenne, as they chased the Cheyenne raiding party away.

The four men halted their horses as the officer in charge rode up to them. "Mister Winslow and Mister Markenson. Glad you made it. We thought maybe you had met your demise, but I see we were wrong. Mister Canfield, thank you for finding them."

Tobias replied first, saying, "T'was nothin', Lieutenant. Glad I found 'em, too."

The lieutenant saw Arapoosh slouching over his pony and asked, "that the Crow scout?"

Jeb answered, "it is."

With lowered eyebrows, the lieutenant said, "he doesn't look so good."

Nate replied, "he ain't, so let's git him to the doctor as soon as possible."

The lieutenant recalled his men, then he and the four men rode to Camp Nelson. Upon entering Camp Nelson, Jeb, Nate, and Tobias breathed a sigh of relief. Jeb looked at Arapoosh, and not liking what he saw, grabbed the reins to Arapoosh's pony, leading him to the makeshift hospital as Jeb and Tobias reined their horses over to headquarters where Major Ivers had just come out to greet them.

As they halted their horses at the hitching rack, Major Ivers stood smiling at them. "Mister Markenson. I'm glad you made it." Looking around, he asked, "And, just where is Mister Winslow and the Crow scout?"

Stepping down from their saddles, Nate answered, "Jeb took Arapoosh to see the doctor just now, Major."

"Leg still bothering him, then?"

"It is," Nate replied. "We had to cauterize it with hot iron a couple days ago to stop the bleeding. I reckon it's still sore from that, plus, he lost a lot of blood before that because of the rough treatment from the Sioux."

"Well, he'll get good treatment now." Giving Nate the once over, Major Ivers said, "you don't look in all that bad shape, Mister Markenson. Did you fair well?"

"More scared than hungry, Major. Not only did we have to worry about Arapoosh screaming out from the hot iron, we had to make sure our fire wasn't noticed. It was a little on the scary side, what with all the Indian war parties around us."

Major Ivers smiled, then said, "well, at least you made..." He stopped, then tilted his head to one side and asked, "you're not gonna want another jug to settle your nerves again, are you, Mister Markenson?"

Nate smiled and chuckled. "No, Major. I've seen all I want from inside the stockade, thank you."

Major Ivers chuckled, then said, "follow me, Gentlemen, to my office. I need a complete detailed report of your... escapades, from when we last seen each other. You as well, Mister Canfield, if you please."

Nate asked, "shouldn't we wait for Jeb as well, Major?"

"I will send for his immediate presence." As they entered headquarters, the major said to the sergeant at the duty desk, "Sergeant Atwater, will you please go to the hospital and tell Mister Winslow, I request his presence in my office?"

"Yes, Sir. Right away, Sir." Sergeant Atwater left headquarters in search of Jeb Winslow.

Shortly, Jeb entered headquarters and the major's office."You want to see me, Major?"

"Yes, Winslow, I do." He paused as he sat behind his desk. "As I was telling these two gentlemen, I need a complete detailed report of your escapades from when we last seen each other. I believe you went in search of, uh, what's his name, again?"

Jeb replied, "Arapoosh, meaning Sour Stomach, Major."

"Yes," Major Ivers replied." Arapoosh. How is his wound, Winslow?"

"Doc says he should be fine in a day or so, which is good news. He's a good man, Major."

"I figured that out when you two took off in order to rescue him from certain death at the hands of the Sioux, Winslow."

Tobias remarked, "he's just another Injun, Major."

Jeb and Nate turned and stared at Tobias, as Major Ivers replied, "and a damned good one, too, Canfield, according to these two, or they wouldn't have done what they did." He paused, then said, "as you are probably aware, if Mister Canfield hasn't already told you, there's a big pow-wow, big medicine, causing a large gathering of the tribes in this area, so we must be ever vigilant in our efforts to protect the settlers, mine workers, and of course, the town of Buffalo Falls from Indian attacks."

All three men replied, "Yes, Sir."

Major Ivers continued. "So, it is with much importance that I have your solemn word that you will assist me in that effort. We have armed the settlers and miners with new weapons and ammunition to ward off those attacks until we can further be reinforced for the Wind River Campaign, and its success." He paused, then said, "I have wired Fort Bridger to be reinforced in that effort. I have yet to have an answer, but I hope very shortly to have an answer to my request. Until then, we do the best we can. Is that understood?"

Jeb replied, "understood, Major."

Major Ivers then asked, "and, do I have your solemn word of your assistance?"

Nate replied, "why would we not, Major? Us helping the Army, is in fact, helping us as well."

Major Ivers smiled. "Very well put, Mister Markenson. Very well put." He interlaced his fingers, then placed his hands on the desk. "And now, Gentlemen, your detailed report, leave nothing out. Tell me, Gentlemen."

Jeb and Nate looked at each other and sighed heavily, then took a seat in the chairs in front of the desk. The only one left standing was Tobias Canfield, who leaned against the wall near the door.

***

In the temporary quarters of Linda Porter, stood Lieutenant Paul Landers, admiring Linda from across the room. He stood, dusty and dirty from the confrontation with the Sioux at the Copper Penny Mining District, and their return to camp Nelson. As he closed the door, she rushed into his arms, buried her head into his chest, wrapping her arms around him, squeezing him roughly, clutching at him vigorously.

He caught the faint aroma of her perfume. "It's so good to be back, Linda. I thought of you every minute."

Without raising her head, she replied, "you lie so sweetly, Paul, but yes, it's so good to have you back with me, too. I was so afraid for your safety." Raising her head to look at him, she said, "I wondered if that would be the last I saw of you, alive, except draped over your saddle as they brought you back to me."

Paul bent down and kissed her roughly. When he released his kiss, he said, "you worry too much. This is my job, Linda, and I am a lieutenant in the US Cavalry, and this is my duty."

"I know, Paul. I know. So, whether I'm here, or back in upstate New York, I'll worry just the same, just as I have since you left New York. Please convey that to Major Ivers."

"I will, Linda, but if he deems it unsafe, for any reason, I have to obey his orders, just as you will, and if he says leave, then you must leave."

Then, the bugler sounded officers call. Paul and Linda both turned to the sound of the bugle until it stopped sounding. "I have to go, Linda, but I promise to talk to Major Ivers about your situation, if I can."

As he released her to arm's length, she said, "thank you, Paul. Thank you."

Again, he kissed her, but gently this time. He released her, turned, and left the room, leaving Linda, again to stare at a closed door.

Lieutenant Landers and every officer in Camp Nelson rushed to headquarters, as Major Ivers came outside, stood waiting to speak. There was overlapping chatter among the officers as they waited for Major Ivers to speak. He looked out over the officers of Camp Nelson, then raising his hands, he said, "Gentlemen, standby for information and orders. I just received communique from Fort Bridger. The reinforcements I requested are not coming. They are needed elsewhere." There was negative reactions among the officers at that news. Major Ivers went on. "So, Gentlemen, it is our responsibility with the remaining man power we have available, to do the best we can, however we can, to protect the settlers and miners in our sector, no matter the cost."

Again, negative comments from the officers of Camp Nelson. The major quieted the officers down, then said, "I intend to do our utmost, full effort, in our duty here at Camp Nelson, for however long it will take, until there are no more hostilities from every Indian tribe in this sector. It may take our bodies in the ground before that happens, but by the Lord God, we will stand tall, squared away, and ever vigilant in our duty." There was an explosion of exaltation and a round of applause at Major Ivers announcement.

It took a few seconds before Major Ivers was able to speak again, but when he did, he said, "Lieutenants Woods, Brentwood, and Landers, my office, please."

They replied, in unison, "Yes, Sir."

Major Ivers, then commanded, "the rest of you, go about your duties as per the duty roster."

Overlapping, "Yes, Sir!" was heard from the officers there.

Jeb, Nate, and Tobias stood off to the side of the formation, listening, leaning against a wall. Jeb, then said, "ain't they purdy?"

Nate turned to Jeb, asking, "ain't who purdy?"

"Those soldier boys in their purdy blue uniforms."

Both Nate and Tobias stared at Jeb, then Nate pushed himself from the wall. "I'm worried 'bout you."

Tobias just shook his head, as he pushed himself away from the wall as well, and walked away.

Jeb stared after them. "Well, they are, ain't they?" He then pushed himself away from the wall and followed them. They went into the makeshift Mess section, looking for a decent meal, other than jerked beef and hard tack.

The aroma of coffee enveloped their nostrils as they said in unison, "oh, that smells so good." They grabbed metal plates, and metal utensils, then filled their plates with whatever was ready. They went and set their plates down at a table, then went after a cup of coffee. They filled their cups and returned, sitting down at the table to eat. There was no conversation as they ate.

Chapter Five

Straws?

In the major's office, Lieutenants Woods, Brentwood, and Landers stood at attention in front of the major's desk, after removing their covers, being inside. Major Ivers seated himself at his desk and looked at the lieutenants assembled in his office. "At ease, Gentlemen."

The three lieutenants replied, "yes, Sir. Thank you, Sir." They stood at parade rest.

Major Ivers turned his attention to Lieutenant Landers. "Lieutenant Landers, it seems Miss Porter is here indefinitely, due to the gathering of tribes in the area. Stage travel has come to a complete halt, and to have her travel otherwise is simply out of the question for her own safety. Any questions, Mister?"

"No, Sir. Linda, I mean, Miss Porter will be satisfied with the news, Major."

"That will be all, Lieutenant, while I talk to these other gentlemen."

"Yes, Sir." With that said, Lieutenant Paul Landers left the major's office.

Major Ivers stood from his desk. "I have left Lieutenant Rutherford at the Copper Penny Mining District to protect the miners from attack. Lieutenant

Woods, you will take your troop and relieve Lieutenant Rutherford, and remain there with the same orders, until you are relieved. Is that understood?"

"Yes, Sir. Understood, Sir."

"You will leave within the hour, Lieutenant. Prepare to leave, Sir."

"Yes, Sir." Stepping back from the desk, he saluted the major, then left the office.

Major Ivers then said, "and you, Lieutenant Brentwood, you will take a troop and leave a day later to relieve Lieutenant Woods from that duty, until you are relieved. Is that understood, Sir?"

Lieutenant Brentwood replied, "understood, Sir."

Major Ivers then said, "that will be all, Lieutenant. Have Sergeant Atwater come in, please? Good day, Sir."

"Yes, Sir. Good day, Sir." He also stepped back from the desk, saluted the major, then left the office.

Then, Sergeant Atwater came into the major's office, standing at attention at the desk. "Yes, Sir?"

Major Ivers said, "Find Winslow, Markenson, and Canfield, and have them report to me as soon as possible, Sergeant, like within the next fifteen minutes."

"Yes, Sir. Right away, Major." With that said, Sergeant Atwater saluted the major, turned and left the office in search of those three individuals. He found them as they came from the Mess and told them the major wanted to see them right away.

Jeb asked, "now, what does he want, Sergeant?"

Sergeant Atwater replied, "I don't know. All I know is, he wants to see the three of you, ASAP."

Nate then said, "well, Fellas, it looks like we're needed, again."

Jeb said, "there's no rest for the weary in this man's Army, is there?"

Nate replied, "it seems not."

Tobias then said, "well, let's go see what the major wants, as if I didn't know."

The three went to headquarters and knocked on the major's door. "Come in, Gentlemen, and have a seat, except for you, Canfield. You'll be leaving as scout for Lieutenant Woods' troop in about forty-five minutes, so prepare yourself to leave."

Tobias replied, "again, Major? I just returned."

"I am very sympathetic to your displeasure, Canfield, but duty calls, seeing you are better rested than Winslow and Markenson at the present time. Their time will soon arrive, I'm sure."

"Okay, Major," Tobias replied, "but, I leave under protest."

Major Ivers replied, "protest duly noted, Canfield."

Tobias turned to look at Jeb and Nate. "You lucky so and so's."

Jeb replied, "his call, Tobias, not ours."

Tobias turned and left the major's office, closing the door behind him, mumbling to himself.

Major Ivers stared at Jeb and Nate, then said, "this I leave to your discretion, Gentlemen. I only need one of you, in twenty-four hours, to go with Lieutenant Brentwood's troop to relieve Lieutenant Woods' troop from the Copper Penny Mining District, leaving on the morrow. I don't really care who it is, or how you decide who it is, but one of you will be going as scout. So, you choose however you prefer."

Jeb replied, "but, Major, we just come from the Copper Penny Mining District, and to tell the truth, there was no pleasure in it. No, Sir."

The major stood slowly to his feet and eyed both Jeb and Nate, quite perplexed, causing them to draw back with raised eyebrows from his stare. "Gentlemen? I am sorely sorry that these Indian attacks have put quite a damper on your pleasure. I will see to it, personally, that you will not have any more pleasure for the next six months, while you're staring out from inside the cells of the stockade. Is that quite understood?" Jeb and Nate stood with their mouths ajar, not knowing what to say, or how to say it. "Is that clear, Gentlemen?"

Nate answered, "Oh, yes, Sir, Major. Quite clear."

Major Ivers pointed to the door of his office, saying quite loudly, "now, get out of my office. The next time I see either of you, is to tell me who's going with Lieutenant Brentwood. Leave. Get... out."

Without saying another word, they both backed up, then turned and left the major's office, closing the door behind them. Just outside the door in the duty room, Jeb asked, "ya think he means it?"

Nate sighed, then said, "I wouldn't press my luck. He's liable to do just that."

The major, hearing what was said just outside his door, replied, "I meant it, Gentlemen."

With that, both men immediately left headquarters in a hurry. The duty sergeant, Sergeant Atwater, looked confused as to what was going on as he watched Jeb and Nate leave headquarters, then turned to the major's door, then back to the door of headquarters. He then shook his head and returned to his paperwork.

Out a ways from headquarters, Jeb turned to Nate. "Ya know? I think he means it."

Nate chuckled as he put his hand on Jeb's shoulder. "Ya know somethin', Jeb? There are times when you plumb worry me." He walked away, saying, "yes, Sir. You just plumb worry me."

Jeb stared after Nate, very much perplexed at what he just said. As Jeb hurried after him to ask what he meant by that remark, they noticed Tobias Canfield leaving the post with Lieutenant Woods' troop on their way to the Copper Penny Mining District. They stood watching for a minute or so, then Nate asked, "just how are we gonna decide who goes and who stays?"

Jeb answered, "I don't rightly know, Nate. Any suggestions?"

"None that I can think of right now. Let's think on it a while."

Jeb said, "that's a good idea. I don't want to worry my mind on such things right now." He then said, excitedly, "how 'bout you and me git us a jug as we think 'bout what the major wants us to do?"

Hesitantly, Nate replied, "uh, no."

"No?" Jeb asked.

Nate said, "yeah. I promised the major we wouldn't, because the last time we had us a jug, we spent the night in the stockade."

Jeb pulled up short, then said, "did you give *our* word to the major, or did you just give *your* word to the major?"

"Well, actually," Nate replied, "I gave *my* word to the major, which, in a way, I gave *our* word to the major."

"Then, you gave only *your* word to the major, meaning I can still git myself a jug, and have a good time."

"You're welcome to try, but I doubt you'll git any results from the major, except a wry grin, and a firm no."

Jeb said, "think so, huh? Well, let's find out, then."

At that, Jeb stormed off toward headquarters and the major's office. Nate found himself a nice shady place to sit to watch the door to headquarters, waiting for Jeb to come out sour-faced and madder than a wet hen. It had taken but a few minutes, but he was correct. Jeb opened the door to headquarters, then slammed it behind him. Nate knew Jeb was angry by the way he acted and carried himself. Then, Jeb saw Nate sitting in the shade chuckling, which caused him to get madder than he was when he came from headquarters. Nate continued to chuckle as Jeb quickly walked off, away from headquarters, and from the sight of Nate.

Nate sat where he was, allowing Jeb time to simmer down. Hopefully, it would be soon, though. They still had to choose which one would be going and which one would stay, that is, as soon as Jeb simmered down. Jeb had disappeared somewhere, but Nate knew Camp Nelson was only so big, and there weren't all that many hiding places for Jeb to hide, which made it all the more comical for Nate. Nate knew Jeb was a logical-minded man, but there were times when, if pressured enough, he would fly off the handle. Sometimes, it took a lot to get Jeb angry, then there were times it was like snapping your fingers, then he was instantly mad, ready to tear your heart out and feed it to the wolves and think nothing more of it than swatting a fly.

***

As Nate sat where he was, he saw the men of Camp Nelson coming off and going on duty at different posts around the camp. He watched as log haulers in their wagons left camp to cut down timbers and bring them here to reinforce the camp. The building of the camp was like watching a fort beginning to build. A new building would soon appear. The enlargement of the camp was beginning to afford new buildings, and a horse arena was even built for roping exercises. Headquarters was even under reconstruction at the rear to expand its office spaces. The hospital was even showing signs of construction. It looked as though Camp Nelson would soon be called Fort Nelson, or whatever the Army deemed it to be, if this should continue.

Nate, then realized it had been close to an hour since Jeb left headquarters, mad as all get out, so he went in search of him, hoping he had simmered down in order to do the choosing. It took but a few minutes to find him. He was at the horse arena watching troopers learn how to rope a horse. As Nate walked up to him, Jeb turned. "What took ya?"

Nate looked confused, then with a crooked smile, asked, "what?"

Jeb chuckled, then said, "I been waitin' a half hour for ya."

"You have?" Nate asked.

"Sure, I have," Jeb replied. "Oh, sure, I was a little ticked off about gittin' no jug, but it didn't take long to simmer down. The major had his reasons for saying no."

Nate smiled widely, then said, "I have misjudged you, Jeb Winslow. I figured it would take you quite a while to simmer down. I was wrong." They lapsed into silence as they watched what was happening inside the arena.

After watching for a few minutes, Jeb finally asked, "have you given more thought as to how to choose?"

"The onliest way I know is to pick straws. The short straw goes with Lieutenant Brentwood. You, uh, you like that idea, do ya?"

Jeb shrugged. "Sure I do but who holds the straw to make it a fair pick?"

Nate answered, "yeah. There's that, huh?" There was silence between them again, then he said, "well, we'll just git three straws then, two long, and one short, then have the major hold 'em. How's that?"

Jeb smiled, saying, "I think ya got somethin' there, Nate. Let's git the straw." They went to the makeshift Livery, took three straws, then headed for headquarters.

Jeb pulled up short and stopped, causing Nate to stop. "What?"

With eyebrows lowered, Jeb asked, "what if the major won't do it?"

"That's easy," Nate replied. "We'll just git someone else to do it."

With raised eyebrows, Jeb chuckled. "Yeah."

And, again off they went to headquarters. When they knocked on the major's door, Major Ivers said, "come in." When they entered, he was sitting at his desk going over some paperwork and had not noticed who it was. When they walked up to the desk, he looked up from his work, and said, "oh, it's you two, and no, you can't have a jug of whiskey."

"Perish the thought, Major," Nate replied. "We need your help."

"Oh?" Major Ivers replied. "And, how can I help you two, this time."

Jeb spoke, saying, "well, seein' as how we're havin' such a hard time decidin' betwixt ourselves, we thought maybe you could help us decide by drawing straws."

Major Ivers drew in a deep breath, then said, "straws. I see." He paused, then said, "don't you think you're a little too old to be playing kids games, Gentlemen? You're grown men playing parlor games. Now, I suggest..."

Nate interrupted the major. "But, Major, we need your help in this matter. Now, all you need to do is make one straw shorter than the other two, and, well, whoever picks the short straw goes with Lieutenant Brentwood to the Copper Penny Mining District tomorrow. See?"

Major Ivers stared at the two with lowered eyebrows, then said, "Straws." Shaking his head, he said, "well, if that will rid you from my office for the day, by gum, I'll do it. Hand me the strands of straw." Nate handed the major the strands of straw and he then turned his back before making one straw shorter than the others. Jeb and Nate tried to see which one was shorter by trying to look around him. Then he turned back around as they straightened up, staring at the strands of straw in his hand. "There you go, Gentlemen, pick one."

Both men looked at the other, then at the straw strands in his hand. Jeb wiped his mouth with his hand, then reached out to pick a straw strand, but drew his hand back. "You pick first, Nate."

Nate replied, "why should I pick first? You almost picked just then, so you pick first."

Major Ivers became a little annoyed. "Oh, for God's sake, one of you just pick. I have urgent paperwork yet to take care of." Both men looked at the strands of straw with raised eyebrows and hesitation. He thrust the strands into Nate's face, demanding, "pick!"

Nate reached out, finally picking a strand.

He then thrust the two straw strands that were left up to Jeb's face, demanding, "pick."

Jeb reached out and picked a strand. Each man inspected the strand they picked, and both were the same size, leaving the smaller strand in the major's hand. Both men smiled at Major Ivers as he sighed a heavy sigh.

Major Ivers tossed the strand of straw away. "Out! Get out! I have better things to do than play parlor games, now get out! Both of you, out!"

As both men were back tracking to the door, Jeb was saying, "but, Major, we need your help with this."

As the major opened the door, he yelled, "Get out!"

When Jeb and Nate were on the other side of the door, they stood staring as the door closed in their faces. Nate turned to Jeb, saying, "if you ask if he meant that, I'll box your ears."

"Who? Me?" Jeb replied. Smirking. "Now, would I do that?"

"As sure as you're born," Nate answered. Then, both men turned and left headquarters. Again, Sergeant Atwater, sitting at the duty desk in the duty room, looked on confused.

Outside headquarters, Jeb and Nate stopped a sergeant, who was walking by and asked him if he would be so kind as to help them make their decision. The sergeant was more than happy to oblige. He was handed the strands of straw and he turned his back, then turned back to Jeb and Nate, holding out the strands.

Nate turned to Jeb. "I chose first last time, so you pick first."

The sergeant asked, "the last time? So, you've done this before?"

Jeb replied, "we have, but it was undecided, cause we both draw'd the same length of strand."

"I see."

Jeb wiped his mouth with his hand, quickly reached out and took a strand of straw. He looked at the straw strand and smiled. Turning to Nate, he said, "your turn. Go ahead. Pick."

Nate quickly reached out and picked a straw strand, then both men compared the strands. Jeb's strand was shorter than Nate's strand.

Jeb tossed the strand away and said, "of all the luck, I had to..."

Nate smiled, then said, "it was done fair and square. Right, Sergeant?"

The sergeant answered, "as fair as could be, Mister."

As the sergeant walked off, Nate said, "see? It was fair."

Jeb replied, "well, there it is, huh?"

Nate placed his hand on Jeb's shoulder. "Now, you have yourself a real good time tomorrow, ya hear? You need to shuffle yourself back into the major's office and tell him you're the one to go with Lieutenant Brentwood tomorrow."

"Yeah," Jeb replied. "I reckon I have to, huh?"

Nate then said, "but, just be careful he don't throw you out on your ear. He was quite unhappy a few minutes ago."

Turning to stare at the door to headquarters, Jeb said, "it can wait a few, I reckon."

"Uh, huh," Nate replied. "Let him simmer down some, huh?"

"Yeah," Jeb answered, as he turned back to Nate. "Let him simmer down some."

Nate then asked, "it couldn't be that you're just a little bit scared of what the major would do, now could it?"

With narrowed eyes, Jeb replied, "who? Me? Scared?" Then, with raised eyebrows, he said, "Could be. Another night in the stockade is not my idea of a good time."

Nate chuckled, then said, "I thought so."

***

Out at the Copper Penny Mining District, Lieutenant Woods had positioned his men at various positions that would afford the best defense against an Indian attack. Tobias Canfield was assigned as scout to give an early warning to the miners, as well as Lieutenant Woods, of an impending attack. Nate really didn't believe they would be attacked. Not now he didn't, what with the big pow-wow, big medicine, and the gathering of tribes. They would be way too busy with dancing and talking among themselves to figure out how to rid the white man from their lands. It seemed their tactics so far had not worked. They knew they needed big medicine, and they believed they had that medicine. The white buffalo.

All the plains tribes urgently needed to find the white buffalo, if it had been born yet, for finding it would mean that prayers to the Great Spirit was being heard, and it was the time for abundance and plenty. The legend of the White Buffalo Calf Woman is known to every tribe on the plains. The celebration could last for days, even a week or more. Tobias Canfield told Lieutenant Woods about the white buffalo, and the legend of the White Buffalo Calf Woman.

Lieutenant Woods remarked, "just superstitious nonsense, if you ask me, Canfield."

"To you and me, it is, but to these Indians, it is not. They believe in different ways. They worship in different ways, and who's to say their Great Spirit isn't the same God we believe in? For instance, these tribes believe that when they dance, it's a form of prayer to the Great Spirit. Most of the celebration of one thing or another, is their way of worship to the Great Spirit for peace or to bring wealth and plenty to the people of the tribe. The drum, in a ceremonial dance, is considered mystical, containing great power, and only a man who had counted coup is eligible to beat the drum. It is held in great esteem and given a place of honor. To us, it's just a drum making a loud noise. So, ya see, Lieutenant, these people may be heathens to us, but to them, we are the heathens who have come to take and then drive them from their lands. They believe no man can own the land. To them, it's Mother Earth, given to them by the Great Spirit."

Lieutenant Woods said, "still, a bunch of gobbledygook to me, Canfield. Just a bunch of superstitious nonsense, and if you think I'm gonna listen to their Great Spirit as..."

Tobias sighed deeply. "Well, it's been fun talkin' to ya, Lieutenant." Then he turned and walked away, leaving Lieutenant Woods to watch after him. Tobias Canfield mounted his horse and rode away from the Copper Penny Mining District, for which he was serving as scout, and an early warning for the miners.

***

Back at Camp Nelson, Jeb had waited a while before he went to see Major Ivers to tell him he was going with Lieutenant Brentwood to the Copper Penny Mining District to relieve Lieutenant Mason Woods and his troop. He entered the major's office and told him the outcome of the picking of straw strands, and how he was chosen for that duty.

Major Ivers sat back in his chair and said, "you look kinda disappointed about that, Winslow."

130

"Well, let's just say I'm not a real big fan of that, Major," Jeb answered. "I came west to become rich and well-to-do, Major, and all I've done so far is dang near git myself killed a time or two."

"Uh, huh," The major replied. "Just where are you from, Winslow? You say you came west. From where? By the way you talk, I'd say, Missouri, Arkansas, maybe."

Jeb replied with pride, "the great Smoky Mountains, Major. Tennessee, to be exact. The Valley of the Three Forks. I come from a family of mountain folk what love to trap, run a trout line. Skinnin', huntin', and trappin' is in our blood, ya might say. Game got kinda scarce back home, 'cept for runnin' a trout line, and a bear ever so often what got caught in a bear trap, so I skedaddled west, and well, here I am."

Major Ivers asked, "how long have you been in this territory, Winslow? Just curious."

Jeb rubbed the back of his neck, looking perplexed, then replied, "oh, I would reckon, nigh onto eight, nine year. I think. Been a spell since I figured that out. Saw no reason to, I expect."

"And, you've kept your hair all this time?" Major Ivers said. "That's quite a feat in and of itself, Winslow."

Jeb chuckled, then said, "it wasn't from lack of tryin' on their part, Major, that's for dang sure."

Major Ivers chuckled, then said, "I suppose not, Winslow."

"What time we leavin' tomorrow?"

Major Ivers answered, "Just before noon. Give you plenty of time to get there, barring any problems."

Jeb said, "You mean Injuns?"

"I do. They've been raiding up and down in this area for quite some time. That's the reason we're here."

"Aw," Jeb answered. "I wouldn't be too worried 'bout 'em now, Major, what with the big pow-wow, the big medicine, and the gatherin' of the tribes. They're dancin' their prayers to the Great Spirit for big medicine. The white buffalo."

"The white buffalo?" the major asked. "And just what will that do for them? Is there such a thing?"

"They haven't found it yet, but that's big medicine to 'em. It means their prayers are being answered by the Great Spirit. Remind me sometime to tell you 'bout the White Buffalo Calf Woman. Quite a story there, and the legend that goes with it."

Major Ivers said, "I'll do that. Sometime. Now, I must ask you to leave, Winslow. I have important matters to attend to."

"You bet, Major," Jeb replied. "And, I'll be ready tomorrow, too."

"Good. Now, if you'll excuse me, I..."

Jeb then said, "oh, yes, Sir, Major. See you tomorrow."

Major Ivers smiled, then said, "thank you, Winslow." Just then, Lieutenant Brentwood came in the opened door of the major's office. "Ah, Lieutenant. We were just talking about you, Sir."

Lieutenant Brentwood replied, "nothing good, I hope, Major. Hello, Jeb."

"Howdy, Lieutenant," Jeb replied.

Major Ivers, then asked, "and just what can I do for you, Lieutenant?"

"I came in to inquire when we'll be leaving, Sir." He smiled, then said, "and to find out which of the two miscreants will be going with me."

Before the major could answer, Jeb spoke. "Miscreants? Why, you bow-legged water moccasin. I am not a miscreant. I am a republican."

Both Major Ivers and Lieutenant Brentwood chuckled over that statement.

Through his chuckling, Major Ivers replied, "just before noon, Lieutenant. It will give you plenty of time to get there, barring..."

Jeb spoke, saying, "Injuns."

Major Ivers said, "yes. Indians or Injuns as Winslow aptly put it."

Lieutenant Brentwood said, "thank you, Sir." Turning to Jeb, he said, "I take it you're going with me, Jeb?"

"Yeah. Unfortunately, I lost at straws."

"Straws?" Lieutenant Brentwood asked, confused.

With a raised eyebrow, Major Ivers shook his head slightly. "Oh, Lieutenant, don't get him started on that. We'll be here 'til you leave tomorrow."

Chuckling, he replied, "yes, Sir."

Lieutenant Brentwood then said, "you be on your best behavior, Jeb. I don't want you falling out of your saddle dead drunk, or I'll toss you in a watering trough to sober you up."

Jeb gave Lieutenant Brentwood a dead pan look, then said, "aw, Lieutenant, you wouldn't do that, would you?"

"As sure as you're born, Jeb." The lieutenant replied.

Major Ivers said, "I don't believe that will be necessary, Lieutenant. He's banned from having a jug. I got his promise from Markenson."

Jeb turned to the major. "Nate didn't give you my promise, Major. He gave you his promise."

"Then, I give you my promise, Winslow. You get no jug. I promise."

Jeb was taken aback by that. "But, Major, that ain't quite fair. Here I am, goin' to risk life, and limb for the welfare of this camp and..."

Major Ivers spoke loudly but smiling, "no jug, Jeb."

Jeb rolled his eyes, shook his head, then said, "now, he calls me, Jeb."

Major Ivers, then said, "Lieutenant, would you please remove this... miscreant from my office, please, Sir?" He smiled.

The lieutenant replied, "yes, Sir." Taking Jeb by the arm, the lieutenant said, "come along, Jeb, just like a good boy."

Jeb said loudly, "I done told you, Lieutenant, I ain't no miscreant. I'm a republican."

The Lieutenant replied, "yeah, you said that already."

As Jeb was ushered to the door, he said, "well, I am."

Major Ivers just chuckled as they left his office and closed the door. He then went back to his paperwork, shaking his head. Outside headquarters, Lieutenant Brentwood and Jeb met Nate Markenson. He was waiting to see if the major would toss Jeb out on his ear. Surprisingly, he did not. He was escorted out by Lieutenant Brentwood.

Nate remarked, "had to call in reinforcements, eh, Jeb?" He chuckled.

Jeb turned to Nate, saying, "Reinforcements?" Jeb pointed to the lieutenant, then said, "him? Naw. He came in as I was gittin' ready to leave. We just walked out together, is all."

Lieutenant Brentwood turned to Jeb, saying, "I expect you to be clean sober when we leave tomorrow, Jeb, or you will rue the day..."

Jeb held up his hand as if calling a halt, then said, "ah, I have no jug of my own, Lieutenant, thanks to Mister, 'I gave my promise', here. Shoot. Can't be anything else but, now can I?"

"Well, I suppose not," Lieutenant Brentwood replied. "I need to be sure of our provisions for tomorrow, so I'll see you tomorrow, then."

"Yeah, sure," Jeb said. "Tomorrow."

Nate said, "I thought for sure the major was gonna throw you out on your ear."

Jeb replied, sarcastically, "well, he didn't, so there, Mister, 'I made a promise'."

Nate shook his head slightly, then said, "you just won't let that be, will ya?"

"Aw," Jeb replied, "I ain't mad. Disappointed, maybe, but I ain't mad." He chuckled, then said, "Could be you and the major was right. I'd most likely be fallin' down drunk, or near to it, and be no good to anybody, includin' my own self. Might git people hurt, or worse. I came to that conclusion all by my lonesome, Mister, 'I made a promise'."

Nate said, "would you stop callin' me that? I'm gittin' an interior complexion, or whatever that dang sayin' is."

Jeb stared at Nate with a raised eyebrow, then said, "okay, I promise."

Nate gave a sour face, then said, "aw, you beat all I ever did see. Ya know that?"

At that said, Nate walked off mumbling to himself, while Jeb just chuckled at him.

As confusion set in, Jeb then said, "danged if I, myself, can remember how that sayin' goes. Oh, well. As the old sayin' goes, 'no hurt, no bird." As he slowly walked away, rubbing the back of his neck, "I think that's how it goes."

Just then, a sergeant walked up to him. "Hey, Markenson."

Jeb turned, replied, "no. I'm Winslow, Sergeant."

The sergeant said, "sorry. Wrong one."

He went to walk away, but Jeb took him by the arm. "What do you mean, wrong one? Wrong one for what?"

The sergeant replied, "don't know, but the major wants him right away, is all I know. You know where I can find him?"

Jeb turned away from the sergeant, saying, "well, I don't rightly know, Sergeant. He was just here a minute ago."

"Well, I need to find him but quick. The major wants him, now."

Jeb replied, "I'll help ya look, Sergeant. He couldn't've gone too far. We'll find him." He headed for the roping arena and corrals, while the sergeant headed for the Mess section. It took but a few minutes to find him. He was coming from the Mess section with a cup of coffee.

The sergeant walked up, asking, "you, Markenson?"

"I am. What's up, Sergeant?"

"The major wants to see you, now, Markenson."

"Yeah?" Nate replied. "What's this about?"

The sergeant replied, "don't know, but he wants to see you ASAP."

"Then, I'm on my way, Sergeant."

With that said, Nate headed for headquarters and the major's office, followed by the sergeant. On their way there, Jeb came up to them. "I see you found him, Sergeant. Didn't hide too hard, did ya, Nate?"

"I wasn't hiding," Nate said. "I went to the Mess for a cup of coffee, and that's where the sergeant found me, so I wasn't hiding. I'm on the way to see the major now."

Jeb said, "I'll go with you."

"Why?" Nate asked.

"Just curious, is all," Jeb replied.

Nate shrugged, "suit yourself."

As they entered headquarters, the duty sergeant, Sergeant Atwater, said, "the major wants to see you, Markenson. What took you?"

"Didn't know he wanted me 'til just a few minutes ago, Sarge, but I'm here now. Nate pointed toward the door. "He in?"

He knocked on the major's door, and the major said, "enter."

Jeb and Nate walked up to the desk, with Nate asking, "you want to see me, Major?"

Major Ivers replied, "I do." He looked at Jeb. "And, just why are you here, Winslow?"

"Just curious, is all, Major."

"I see. Well, this doesn't concern you, Winslow, but you're welcome to stay, if you so desire."

"I doth desire, Major." Jeb smiled.

Major Ivers said, "uh, huh. Well, anyway, I need you, Markenson to scout for Captain Carmichael."

Nate replied, "oh?"

"Yes," Major Ivers answered. "He's leading a six-wagon, wagon train to collect much needed supplies from a wagon train coming from Fort Bridger. You will meet them a little over half way at a place called Council Bluffs. Know where that is, Markenson?"

Nate answered, "I do, Major."

"The Shoshone are pretty thick in that area, and I need you to go as Captain Carmichael's scout on their journey."

Jeb said, "there's a Shoshone reservation close to Council Bluffs, but they pay no never mind to it, until winter when they eat Army beef."

Nate asked, "When do we leave, Major?"

The major replied, "they are not even half way yet, from the wire I received, so you'll leave come daylight, Markenson, and good luck."

Nate asked, "does, Captain...?"

Major Ivers answered, "he does. I just informed him a few minutes ago, while waiting for you."

"All right, Major," Nate replied. "I'll be ready."

"Good," Major Ivers said, "get some sleep, Markenson. Good day, Gentlemen."

Both men, then said, "good day, Major."

***

Just before dawn the next morning, Captain Carmichael, his six-wagon supply train, plus a twenty-man guard, and Nate Markenson as scout, left Camp Nelson to meet up with the six-wagon supply train coming from Fort Bridger at a place called Council Bluffs. It would take no less than three days to reach Council Bluffs. Captain Carmichael's orders were to bring the loaded wagons to Camp Nelson, as the empty wagons return to Fort Bridger. Jeb stood by the gate, smiling at Nate, telling him to be careful. Nate promised he would, and for Jeb to do the same as he went with Lieutenant Brentwood to the Copper Penny Mining District to relieve Lieutenant Mason Woods from their duty. Jeb also promised he would be careful. Then, the gate to Camp Nelson closed behind them.

Just before noon the same day, Jeb mounted his horse and sat beside Lieutenant Brentwood as they prepared to leave Camp Nelson for the Copper Penny Mining District. Just then, a trooper was announced at the gate from post number one, but before entering, the trooper fell from his horse. The gate swung open by the command of Lieutenant Brentwood, then he and Jeb quickly dismounted. Rushing to the trooper, they looked around themselves for any signs of danger. The trooper was in terrible condition. His clothes were tattered and torn. He had suffered the wound of an arrow to his left side and it was still protruding from him. Lieutenant Brentwood and Jeb quickly picked him up and swung his arms over their necks and rushed him into camp.

Major Ivers ran to the gate as the lieutenant and Jeb, with the trooper, came rushing in. The trooper had passed out. Water was the brought to revive him, if they could. They needed to find out who, what, when, and where he suffered this arrow wound. They splashed water onto his face at least three times before he gave a reaction. Major Ivers said, "Good, he's coming around. Take him to hospital and get as many answers you can from him." He turned to Sergeant Elmer Daniels, the duty sergeant. "Sergeant, find Lieutenant Landers, and have him meet me in the hospital right away. He may be needed, somewhere."

"Yes, Sir. Right away, Sir."

Within a few minutes, Lieutenant Landers and Linda Porter arrived at the hospital. "Lieutenant Landers reporting as ordered, Major."

Major Ivers turned and saw Linda Porter had come with him. "And, why are you here, Miss Porter? I only requested the lieutenant here."

Then, Major Ian Talley, MD, and Surgical Staff asked, "Miss Porter, I hear you're a nurse. Is this true?"

"I was at one time, Doctor. Yes."

The doctor said, "Good. I have other patients, as you can see, please do what you can for them, and assist where you can while I tend to this man, if you please."

Major Ivers spoke, "Ian, she is not an Army nurse and having her tend to these other patients is against Army regulations."

"A nurse is a nurse, no matter the Army regulations, Mark, and as you can see, I'm in need of a qualified nursing assistant, and from what I hear, she'll do just fine."

Lieutenant Landers and Linda Porter stared at Major Ivers for a long few seconds, then the major motioned with his head and a sigh, giving his permission. They turned to each other, smiling, then Linda eagerly went about her task the doctor had given her, as Lieutenant Paul Landers looked on smiling.

Major Ivers, then asked, "was he able to answer any questions, Ian? He was coming around out at the gate. We need to know what he knows about that arrow."

"Not yet, Mark," Ian answered. "I'm afraid he'll be out a while. Until then, that arrow will remain a mystery."

Major Ivers sighed heavily and being frustrated at the events, he turned to Lieutenant Landers. "Be ready to leave at a moments notice, Lieutenant. When he comes around, we'll know."

Chapter Six

Attack! Attack!

Near Council Bluffs, there is a settlement called Alderwood, just a few miles from the Shoshone Indian reservation. A few miles from Alderwood, five trappers were attacked by Indians. Two men were killed instantly, one man severely injured, and unable to move, while the last man ran for his life with a few Indians in pursuit. Coming to the Wind River, the man jumped into the water at a shallow point of the river among the reeds, bulrushes, weeds, and bare roots of Willow and Alder trees growing along the bank of the river. He frantically cut a few reeds to the desired length, then lowered himself into the water with the reeds in his mouth with the tops of those reeds just above the water to supply him with air. He reached out, grabbing a root of a Willow tree to hold himself under the water, hidden among the roots of trees.

The Indians searched, but could not find him. After what seemed like hours, the man slowly raised himself from the water among the reeds, bulrushes, and weeds. He listened for any sign of danger, but heard nothing but the rushing of water. He raised himself farther from the water, surveyed the area and found the Indians had left. He made his way to Alderwood, and the whole settlement went into an uproar. Soon, a thirty-man mob, armed to the teeth, mounted and headed for the Shoshone

Reservation, believing they were the ones who attacked these men. With hate in their hearts, and narrowed eyes, they rode steadfast, with only one thought on their minds – revenge.

When the six-wagon supply train, commanded by Captain Carmichael, was between Alderwood and the Shoshone Indian Reservation, the thirty-man mob came towards the supply wagons at a dead run. Captain Carmichael, believing they were being attacked, started yelling orders to defend themselves. The troopers readied themselves against the attack. Then, the thirty-man mob came to a halt fifty yards from the supply wagons. One of the men in front, raised his rifle in the air sideways. Captain Carmichael then told his men to stand down. Then, with great reluctance, he rode out to talk to the thirty-man mob. When he was at least ten yards from those men, he stopped. With anger in his voice, he asked, "what's wrong with you? We almost fired on you thinking we were being attacked."

"Sorry, Captain," came the reply. "We're on our way to the Injun reservation to teach these Injuns they can't just go around killin' people. Five men were attacked, two were killed outright. One severely injured, and now dead. The last man came into Alderwood and explained what had happened, and we're on our way to git a little revenge."

Captain Carmichael asked, "and what makes you think the Shoshone had anything to do with that attack?"

The man sat uneasy in the saddle, then said, "it couldn't be anyone else but, Captain. The Shoshone reservation isn't far from here, and...."

Just then, Nate Markenson came riding up to them. "What's goin' on here, Captain?" When he was told what happened, and why these men were here, he replied, "well, Captain, the Shoshone indeed could be the ones what did that raid."

The man in front then said, "see there, Captain?"

Then, there came uneasy rumblings from the thirty-man mob. Then Nate said, "but, I doubt it."

Amidst the grumblings of that last statement, the man in front, said, "what?"

Nate replied, "there have been Sioux in the area, and not far from where you said the attack occurred against those five men."

Captain Carmichael then asked, "are you sure, Markenson?"

"Dead sure, Captain," Nate answered.

The man in front, then asked, "how do you know?" Nate turned to stare at him without answering. The man asked again, in a louder tone of voice, "how do you know?"

Nate sighed, then said, "I seen 'em. About a dozen or more, lookin' for trouble, and I wasn't goin' to oblige 'em, either. I kept my distance until I could no longer see or hear 'em. Now you know."

Captain Carmichael then said, "well, Mister, you could have made a grave mistake. These Injuns, as you put it, are on a reservation the US government has set aside for them, so until we know who actually did that murderous raid, I warn you not to go any farther until facts are known, and those facts are satisfactory to the Army, then whoever it was will be punished by law."

The man in front then said, "to the Army? By law? These men were civilians, Captain, not...."

Captain Carmichael replied, rather heatedly, "I am well aware of that, Mister. That is why the Army is in this sector, to try to put down Indian attacks, and supply settlers in this area with updated arms and ammunition against Indian attacks."

The man in front smiled, grumbling, then said, "and just where was the Army when those men were attacked, Captain? Playin' mumbletypeg?"

That questioned caused jubilations from the thirty-man mob, but caused Captain Carmichael and Nate to be insulted. Nate smiled, then asked, "shall I shoot him, Captain, for being insolent?"

Captain Carmichael smiled, then answered, "no, Markenson. That would be murder."

The man in front gritted his teeth, then said, "you wouldn't dare!"

Captain Carmichael turned to Nate, saying, "But, we could shoot him for his stupidity, though."

The man in front remarked, "There are thirty of us, captain, and, they are witnesses."

Captain Carmichael turned to the man. "And, there are twenty of the finest marksmen in the Army, under cover, so who do you think will win? Me and my men, or you and your men?"

Both Nate and the captain sat smiling at the man in front. The man in front began to fidget on his saddle, as he looked at the men in the wagons with their weapons trained on them.

Captain Carmichael, then asked, "well, Mister, shall we shoot it out?"

"You're here to protect and serve, Captain, not to commit murder."

Captain Carmichael smiled, then said, "your death and the death of most of your men can easily be explained, Mister. You came riding hell bent for leather towards our supply wagons, and we thought we were under attack and fired, in self-defense, of course. And, understandably, you and your men fired back in self-defense, but the damage had already been done, and who do you think the Army will believe when I give my report?"

The man in front readily agreed, saying, "you and your report, I reckon." The thirty-man mob grumbled their displeasure, but turned their horses and headed back towards Alderwood, but kept looking back over their shoulders as if they didn't trust the Army.

Captain Carmichael said, "well, Markenson, it looks as though they don't trust us."

Nate chuckled, saying, "so, it would seem, Captain. So, it would seem."

Captain Carmichael then asked, "did you really see the Sioux out there, or were you just saying that for those men?"

"Yes, Captain, I really saw Sioux out there," Nate replied. "Not as many as I said, but yes, there are Sioux out there."

Captain Carmichael said, "and, yet, there is no evidence that either the Shoshone or the Sioux attacked those men, but someone did. My money is on the Sioux."

Nate replied, "I reckon we'll never know, Captain, without evidence."

"That is a sad history, but a true statement." They turned their horses back to the wagons, then Captain Carmichael said, "well, let's continue on, shall we?" As they rode back to the wagons, he asked, "just how much further until we reach Council Bluffs?"

"Four more miles. Just beyond that ridge yonder."

The captain asked, "have you checked out Council Bluffs to know whether or not the wagons are there yet?"

"I was on my way when I noticed that little jaw session you were havin'."

The captain then said, "well, we'll stop about a mile out, and wait for your word that they're there. I do not want to be surprised, Markenson, nor go back with empty wagons."

"Understood, Captain. I'll go have a look see." With that said, Nate reined his horse away from the captain and headed for Council Bluffs.

Soon the six-wagon wagon train was again underway.

Within a mile or so from Council Bluffs, Nate came riding full gallop back to the wagons, shouting, "Cheyenne, Captain. They're layin' waste to the wagon train from Fort Bridger."

Captain Carmichael began shouting, "Corporal Munson, you and three men stay here and guard the wagons. The rest follow me and Markenson. We have Cheyenne to contend with at Council Bluffs."

Corporal Munson replied, "yes, Sir."

Then, the rest of the troop hurriedly took out for Council Bluffs to route out the Cheyenne attacking the wagon train from Fort Bridger. Captain Carmichael and the troopers came charging into the fray, alarming the Cheyenne in their attack, causing most of them to run from the field of battle. Gun smoke hung heavy in the air. Dead and dying Cheyenne, as well as troopers littered the ground. A lieutenant appeared from behind a barricade, dirty and disheveled, firing his service weapon at the departing Indians. He was shouting almost maniacally, as he fired his weapon at them. It took three times for Captain Carmichael shouting at him, to get his attention. When his weapon finally landed on an empty chamber, the lieutenant turned to Captain Carmichael, almost in tears. As Captain Carmichael dismounted, he said, "get your wits about you, Lieutenant."

"But, Captain...?"

Captain Carmichael said, "I know, Lieutenant, but you need to keep your wits about you."

Nate reined his horse in beside the captain's horse, then said, "we skedaddled 'em, Captain. We showed 'em what for."

Knowing the mental state of the lieutenant, Captain Carmichael turned to a sergeant nearby. "Sergeant, I need a casualty list as soon as possible."

"Yes, Sir."

Captain Carmichael, then asked, "who's second in command, Sergeant?"

The sergeant looked around himself, then said, "I reckon I am, Captain. Second Lieutenant Fleming is dead, Sir."

Captain Carmichael then said, "I am sorry for your loss, Sergeant. I will allow a full day's rest before I allow you to return to Fort Bridger."

The sergeant replied, "thanks, Captain. We surely could use it. What of Lieutenant Ackerman?"

Captain Carmichael sighed, then said, "hopefully, a day's rest will be a good thing for him, Sergeant."

"Yes, Sir."

Then Captain Carmichael turned to Nate. "Mister Markenson, if you would please, go bring in our wagons for transfer, while I form a burial detail."

"Alright, Captain." Nate reined his horse away from the captain and headed for the wagons to be brought in.

Captain Carmichael then started barking orders to the men who were there to form a burial detail. He then took Lieutenant Ackerman by the arm and led him to shade and ordered water for him.

Lieutenant Ackerman ran his fingers through his hair, then said, "I'm fine, now, Captain. I have my wits about me. Those Indians scared the holy hell right outta me. I guess I lost it, huh?"

Captain Carmichael replied, "I would say so, Lieutenant, but with good cause. Your men were very afraid for their lives themselves. The very thought of having your life taken from you is very frightening."

Lieutenant Ackerman then said, "I didn't make a good showing of myself with my men, and I can understand that. If this were to happen again, and with me in command, will they trust me?"

Captain Carmichael answered, "that will only be answered by the men under your command, Lieutenant. However you do it, you need to earn back the respect of your men."

"I agree with you, Captain," Lieutenant Ackerman replied, "but how do I do that?"

***

Out at the Copper Penny Mining District, it has been three days since Jeb and Lieutenant Brentwood relieved Lieutenant Mason Woods of his duty. The miners going about their work was the only thing going on. Jeb would scout about a mile, around about, and yet, he found no reason for alarm. Lieutenant Brentwood took up the same positions Lieutenant Woods had taken against an attack. For three days, no cause for alarm. Not an Indian could be found anywhere near the copper mine. Traffic to and from the town of Garden City was uninterrupted. To Jeb, it was down right spooky. The big pow-wow. The big medicine, and the gathering of the tribes went into effect about the same time they relieved Lieutenant Woods. How long would that last?

***

At Camp Nelson and the trooper who collapsed at the gate and taken to the hospital, had finally came to his senses and was awake. Major Ivers had been made aware of it and requested Lieutenant Landers to meet him in the hospital. Sergeant Daniels again went in search of

Lieutenant Landers. Linda Porter was still in the hospital helping Major Talley where she could.

Major Talley said to Linda, "you have been a great help, Miss Porter, and I would like to thank you for your assistance. Thank you."

"That is quite unnecessary, Major, for it was a pleasure. It all came back to me of what I was trained to do. I really should thank you for that."

Just then, Major Ivers, as well as Lieutenant Landers, and Sergeant Daniels, entered the hospital. They walked over to where the trooper lay with his head resting on a down pillow on his clapboard bed. Major Ivers asked, "it's been a few hours, Ian. Is he able to answer questions?"

"I should think so, Mark," the doctor replied. "But, only a few for now. He'll need plenty of rest for a while, but I'm afraid there's no hope for him."

Major Ivers knelt down, then said, "Trooper, can you tell me when and where you got that arrow? Was it an attack on a wagon train, or was it elsewhere?"

The trooper had labored breathing, and he languished in his effort to speak. Then, just above a whisper, he said, "Alpine Meadows. Indians. People - dead. Attack."

Then, he went limp. The doctor checked the man for signs of life, then shook his head. "He's dead, Mark. Poor fellow."

Major Ivers turned to Lieutenant Landers. "Alpine Meadows? That's a settlement I've not heard of before, Lieutenant. Do you know where this Alpine Meadows is located?"

Lieutenant Landers replied, "yes, Sir. It's almost a day's ride from here, back up into the Big Horn Mountains, Major."

"Gather your troop, Lieutenant, and head for the Big Horn Mountains. Find Alpine Meadows. Assist where assistance is needed."

Lieutenant Landers replied, "yes, Sir."

"And, Lieutenant? If there are none alive, hightail it back here. Is that understood?"

Lieutenant Landers answered, "yes, Sir."

Paul Landers gave Linda Porter a look of endearment. Linda returned the look, then watched him hurry away.

Major Ivers turned to her to say something, then changed his mind, turned from her, as he, himself, hurried away. Out in front of headquarters, Lieutenant Landers had gathered his troop, and was preparing to leave. As Major Ivers stood and watched, he was overcome with a great weight that seemed to be leveled on his shoulders. Then, he heard Lieutenant Landers yell, "Troop! Forward! Ho!" Then, they left Camp Nelson at a slow gait. Then, outside the gate, the lieutenant pumped his arm up and down, and they troop took to a fast gait. Within a few minutes, the sentries on the parapets could no longer see them, as they disappeared into the trees and hills around Camp Nelson.

Major Ivers wished he could be leading the troop, but his presence was needed here, plus he had so much paperwork to do. He chuckled knowing he didn't have Nate Markenson and Jeb Winslow to interrupt him on an almost hourly basis. Then, he found himself saying, aloud to himself, "Straws!" Then, he said aloud, "Be careful, Lieutenant. Be thyself careful."

***

Lieutenant Landers knew that in the Big Horn Mountains there were tribes of Crow, Arapaho, Ute, Kiowa, Arikara, the Blackfeet, and possibly a few more he wasn't aware of, so he cautiously led his troop into the Big Horn Mountains at a steady gait. Indian scouts were sent out, and so were outriders. As the trail led high into the mountains, the troop snaked around and around, then up and down. The trail had switchbacks that led higher into the mountains. Then, all of a sudden, the trail emptied out onto a high plateau. As they followed it, about a mile later, they came to the outskirts of Alpine Meadows, almost enclosed by Alpine trees. There, the lieutenant halted his troop as the scouts came back to the troop all flustered.

Through an interpreter, he was informed there were none alive and bodies were lying everywhere. He was also told it had been the Blackfeet who had attacked the settlement. Lieutenant Landers then said, "Sergeant

Wallace, with me. The rest stay put." With that said, he, Sergeant Wallace, and the scouts rode at a fast gait into the settlement of Alpine Meadows. As they rode the main street of the settlement, they saw men, women, and children lying dead, as well as Blackfeet Indians. The white men had been scalped. The women were stripped and could only be assume they had been abused before they died. How many women and children had been carried away by the Blackfeet was unknown. Boys above the age of ten had their heads bashed in, or they died in some other manner.

The sight was horrendous and the smell of death lingered. When they rode back to the troop, Lieutenant Landers turned to look back at the settlement. "There are too many to take the time to bury." Turning back to the troop, he said, "let's head back to Camp Nelson. The Blackfeet may still be in the area."

Sergeant Wallace said, "That's a sight I will never forget, Lieutenant. Never."

"I've seen a few such sights, Sergeant, but you never get used to it. At times, things like this can make your skin crawl. I know mine does."

Sergeant Wallace responded, "makes me want to take a bath. I feel so dirty just lookin' at it."

"I know the feeling, Sergeant." Going to the head of the troop, Lieutenant Landers yelled, "Troop, let's go home." He made a full right turn going back to Camp

Nelson. Scouts and outriders were sent out. They rode, ever vigilant of the danger that could be all around them or waiting just up ahead. He yelled back to the troop, "carbines at the ready."

Each man removed his carbine from its boot and rested the butt against his leg, barrel up, or across their saddles as they rode, searching the area for signs of danger. Soon, they began their descent down the winding, twisting trail that led out of the mountains.

When they had reached the foothills, they saw a stage, not far away, running wild with Indians chasing after it. Gunshots were heard as the shots echoed across the land. Lieutenant Landers yelled, "Troop at a gallop, charge."

The troop took off, trying to get between the stage and the Indians. They raced at the Indians, firing their carbines. Firing from the stage continued, as the Indians hesitated their assault. Indians were falling from their ponies as the troop engaged in the assault. The Indians pulled back from their attack, veering off, away from the troopers, shouting and shooting as they left. The stage driver tried as hard as he could, but could not stop the horses. The horses were out of control, and he could not stop them.

Sergeant Wallace raced to the leaders, grabbed the closest one's head gear and began to pull on it as he began to slow his own horse. This maneuver slowed the horses down to where they could finally be stopped. As the stage rocked back and forth from its sudden stop, the passengers began to pile out and the driver climbed down from the seat still holding his rifle. Lieutenant Landers reined in beside the stage, then shortly, he was joined by Sergeant Wallace.

Lieutenant Landers turned to Sergeant Wallace, saying, "good work, Sergeant."

"Thank you, Sir."

As Lieutenant Landers stepped down from the saddle, he asked, "is everyone okay?"

There were four men and two women on the stage, but only three men stood outside. The two women were near hysterics, eyes ever moving, looking for more danger. The driver noticed, then asked, "where's that other gentleman? That portly fella with the brown derby hat?"

One of the men replied, "I'm afraid he didn't make it. He's dead, leaning against the other door."

The driver said, "that's too bad. He was a likable fella." Turning to Lieutenant Landers, he said, "boy, am I glad you fellas showed up when you did, Lieutenant."

Taking his Winchester, he cocked it, showing the lieutenant he had no more ammunition. The only weapons that were still working was from inside the coach. Then, the passengers began to thank the lieutenant for coming to their rescue.

Lieutenant Landers replied, "well, thank you, but it was lucky for you we were in the area."

One of the women said, "God works in mysterious ways, Lieutenant. He sent us you in our time of *great* need." She reached and softly caressed his face, saying, "bless you, Lieutenant."

Lieutenant Landers touched the brim of his hat, then replied, "yes, Ma'am. Thank you, Ma'am." Sergeant Wallace looked at the lieutenant with a smirk and with the eyes of a skeptic. The lieutenant looked up at Sergeant Wallace with a raised eyebrow, then the sergeant averted his eyes, looking around at nothing. "Are you able to continue without an army escort, Driver? The troop has pressing news for Major Ivers at Camp Nelson."

"I can, if those dad blasted Injuns leaves us alone, I can."

Lieutenant Landers replied, "Good. Then, I'll not keep you any longer."

The driver asked, "What about that portly fella, Lieutenant? I can't take him along with us, him bein' dead and all, what with the women."

Lieutenant Landers sighed, then said, "leave him. We'll bury him."

The driver nodded his head, then said, "alright, Gents, let's drag him outta there." Two men went to the other side of the stage and dragged the dead man out and laid him on the ground, away from the stage. They gave

Lieutenant Landers a foreboding look. "Thank you, Lieutenant, for buryin this fella."

"It needs done, Driver." Turning to Sergeant Wallace, the lieutenant ordered a burial detail.

"Yes, Sir."

Then, as each person boarded the stage, they again thanked the lieutenant for coming to their rescue. Lieutenant Landers kept saying, "You're welcome. You're welcome," to each person." As the driver took his seat on the stage, he yelled, "catch, Driver." Then he threw a couple boxes of 44.40 caliber ammunition up to the driver, one at a time.

The driver caught both boxes, smiled and said, "thanks, Lieutenant. These, most likely, will come in mighty handy." Before he got the stage underway, he loaded the Winchester with the ammunition. He then took up the reins and slapped them over the backs of the draft horses, shouting, "giddy-up. Yee-haw. Git along, hosses." Clicking his teeth, he shouted, "Giddy-up, hosses." As the staged rocked back and forth from its sudden forward movement, the men and women waved goodbye, leaving Lieutenant Landers to watch after them, smiling at their leaving. He was joined by Sergeant Wallace who also watched the stage rattle away. Lieutenant Landers, turned, mounted his horse, then asked, "how long, Sergeant?"

Sergeant Wallace replied, "not long, Captain. Soft ground."

With the portly fellow finally buried, along with a couple of troopers who had lost their lives, Sergeant Wallace said, "I hope these men will not be forgotten, Lieutenant."

"As long as they're recorded in my report, Sergeant, they won't be."

Sergeant Wallace replied, "Yes, Sir."

Crude wooden crosses were placed at the head of each grave, unmarked. The portly fellow had no papers of any kind as to his identity, so his grave went unmarked as well as the troopers who were buried. Thwarting the Indian assault on the stage had taken close to two miles, much to the dismay of Lieutenant Landers.

He asked, "what say we go home now, Sergeant?"

Sergeant Wallace smiled and replied, "yes, Sir!"

Reforming in lines of two abreast, the lieutenant said, "Troop! Let's go home." They turned and headed back towards Camp Nelson, hoping not to encounter any more Indian hostilities.

***

With Captain Carmichael and his troop at Council Bluffs exchanging supply wagons from Fort Bridger, Lieutenant Brentwood and his troop away at the Copper Penny Mining District, and Lieutenant Landers and his troop away at Alpine Meadows, in the Big Horn Mountains, Camp Nelson was under a skeleton crew. Thank goodness Lieutenant Mason Woods and his troop were here, or Major Ivers would have thought he had been abandoned at his post. Without Lieutenant Woods and his troop here at camp, there was only Lieutenant Darrell Hollis with his troop. The major dreaded the thought of the camp being attacked with what little man power that was available to him. It could mean utter destruction for Camp Nelson.

Linda Porter came from the hospital to get some fresh air and relax a little. It seemed she had been in the hospital for hours, tending to the sick and wounded. Doctor Major Ian Talley told her to leave and get some rest, as she deserved it. Outside the hospital, leaning against a post, she noticed Major Ivers out in front of headquarters, his hands folded behind his back, pacing back and forth. She pushed herself away from the post and wandered over to him. As she walked up to him, she noticed he was preoccupied and had not noticed her. She stood and measured this man of importance a few seconds.

Then, the major acknowledged her presence by asking, "Miss Porter, you have questions?"

"You seem troubled, Major. Problems?"

Major Ivers replied, "plenty, but none that you should be concerned with, Miss Porter. Worried is the word for the day, I'm afraid."

"I've been too busy to be worried, Major. I have the time now to be worried. I'm very worried about Paul. That would be, Lieutenant Landers, Major."

Major Ivers said, "I'm aware of who you mean, Miss Porter. Quite aware of it. Maybe we can worry together, but for different reasons?"

"Or, maybe the same reasons, Major," Linda said. Major Ivers glanced over at her, as she said, "I rather believe you are quite fond of all the officers and men under your command."

"Fond of them, Miss Porter?" Major Ivers asked. "I am quite fond of them. I am proud to serve with such caliber of men as these. These men show gallantry above and beyond the call of duty. Fond of them? Yes, I'm very fond of them."

"I can see it in your eyes at times, Major. It is very appealing; how much you do care for your men."

Major Ivers asked, "it shows that much, huh? And, here I thought I hid it quite well."

"As the saying goes, Major, the eyes are the window to the soul, and you have an endearing one."

"Endearing, huh? Well, let's just let that be our little secret, shall we, Miss Porter?"

Linda smiled, chuckling, then said, "as you wish, Major. Our little secret, it is."

"Thank you."

Linda replied graciously, "you're welcome."

Major Ivers turned to look at her. "If I were only fifteen years younger, why, I'd give Lieutenant Landers a run for his money at getting your affection away from him."

Linda was taken aback by that statement, and replied, "how sweet of you, Major. Thank you."

***

Jeb Winslow was riding just under a mile from the Copper Penny Mining District when he suddenly halted his horse. He seen something that caught his eye, and he was none too happy about it, either. He reined his horse into the trees for cover. Some distance away from him, he saw a band of Indians coming from over a hill in his direction. He studied their markings and their dress, then became instantly afraid. They were not Sioux, Cheyenne, Arapaho, or Blackfeet Indians. These were Pawnee Indians. They were hunter-gatherers, but most recently, they were war-like against anything white. He reckoned they came from the southern Sawtooth Mountain range on a hunt. They were hunting, all right. Hunting the white man and gathering their scalps. Jeb waited 'til they were out of sight, then reined his horse back towards the mine to inform Lieutenant Brentwood of what he had seen.

Lieutenant Brentwood was sitting in his camp chair writing his obligatory troop report when he saw Jeb riding, hell bent for leather, back to the mining district.

Curiosity took hold of him as he stood and waited for Jeb to arrive. When Jeb had reached him, he reined in short, then dismounted.

With a raised eyebrow, Lieutenant Brentwood asked, "trouble, Jeb?"

"And, how, Lieutenant! Comin' almost any time now."

"Sioux?"

Jeb answered, "nuh, uh. Pawnee."

The lieutenant turned and started shouting orders. The men at the mine were put on alert, so they gathered their weapons and found cover. Under cover, they waited for what seemed like hours, but was only a few minutes until they saw their first of many Pawnee warriors coming through the trees. The Pawnee just sat their ponies a hundred yards or so from them. They were searching the area, chatting between themselves and pointing, probably wondering why there were no miners. The sun glistened and shined through the trees, bouncing off the miner's metal carts and what-not, that to the Pawnee, it looked as if the light bounced off hidden rifle barrels.

Because of the light infraction, they gave a war cry and charged the mine. As they came screaming at them, the miners opened with a volley of gun shots that rang as one huge weapon against the Indians. Warriors began falling from their ponies as the Indians began shooting back at the miners with arrows and bullets. Lieutenant

Brentwood became quite angry the miners fired without having the order to do so, so he ordered his men to fire. Firing all at once, the troopers caused a moment of hesitation on the assault. The assault gained momentum for at least another fifteen minutes. Then, the Pawnee disengaged from the assault and rode back to a safe distance, turning their ponies back to the miners.

Lieutenant Brentwood shouted, "hold your fire, men, until they're close enough to shake hands!"

Jeb's facial expression changed from extreme concern to a raised eyebrow, as he turned to the lieutenant. "Shake hands? I don't expect to git that friendly, Lieutenant."

"That's just an expression, Jeb."

Jeb replied, "and, I expressed my opinion on the matter." His eyes widened as he yelled, "here they come again!"

The Pawnee charged with greater enthusiasm than that of the last charge and with more intensity.

In the last charge, no one was killed but Pawnee. This charge was a might different. There was more of a reason, other than killing a white man. Revenge! This charge was revenge for the warriors who were killed in the last charge. Probably relatives lay dead or dying in the dirt. This had put a new reasoning in the hearts of the Pawnee. They charged. This time, the miners waited for the order to fire from Lieutenant Brentwood, and when he did give that order, the mine exploded with firepower. Ponies as well as Pawnee lay dead or dying in the dirt. No other casualties occurred, either to the miners or the troopers. The Pawnee limped from the field of battle with their tails stuck between their legs.

The land at the mining district was littered with dead and dying Pawnee warriors. The miners leaped for joy at defending themselves. Without giving any rise to the actions of the miners, Lieutenant Brentwood turned a blind eye to them who went around mercy killing the Pawnee who were just lying there, wounded. To Jeb, the sight was appalling, and he made his complaint known to the lieutenant very clearly.

Lieutenant Brentwood rebuffed Jeb's complaint. "What's the matter, Jeb? Pawnee scalps aren't good enough for you? You had no complaint at Cedar Creek, now did you?"

Jeb stood fuming at the lieutenant. Choosing his words carefully, he said, "those were Sioux, Lieutenant. These are Pawnee. And, as far as I know, they never did me no wrong, until today."

Lieutenant Brentwood replied, angrily, "scalps are scalps, Winslow. Take them or not. Those are the fortunes of war. I, myself, think it's appalling, taking scalps, but, but you do what you want. Scalps are scalps, Winslow, and it's sickening!"

Jeb replied, angrily, "and killing wounded Indians ain't?" As Jeb abruptly turned and angrily walked away, Lieutenant Brentwood, shouted after him, saying, "they would do the same thing to us, Jeb, then give us an Indian haircut."

Angrily, Jeb mounted his horse and rode away, leaving the mining district behind him.

On foot, Lieutenant Brentwood went running after him, shouting, "Winslow! Winslow! Jeb? Come back here!" Then, making a cone with his hands on his mouth, he shouted, "Winslooow!"

Jeb rode about a half mile out, then halted his horse, and sat there stewing in his own anger. He was upset at what happened at the mine. Shooting wounded Indians was not what Jeb had agreed to. It was true he didn't partake in that, but he felt he allowed it, and that unnerved him and made him angry. He reasoned within himself that what happened at the mine was out of his control. He had made his complaint to Lieutenant Brentwood, but it went nowhere. He turned a blind eye to it, and that bothered him immensely. He was so immersed in his own anger, he had not heard the rustling in the brush. When he finally became aware of it, it was too late. He was swept off his horse by an Indian.

Both began tugging and pulling at each other to gain a better foothold against the other. When they separated and came to their feet, the Indian pulled his knife, and then they began circling each other. The Indian made a cutting slash at Jeb, who quickly backed away from the knife. Jeb's eyes went from the knife to the feet of the Indian, then back to the knife in his hand.

Again, the Indian made a slashing move with the knife, from which Jeb quickly backed away. The Indian made a stabbing move toward Jeb, and he caught his knife hand and tossed him away from him. The Indian lost his footing and Jeb charged him, catching him in the stomach with his shoulder, then they both went sprawling into the dirt.

The Indian tried to maneuver his knife to stab Jeb, but with Jeb on top of him, Jeb had grabbed his knife hand and began slapping it against the ground. Finally, the knife flew from the Indian's hand, letting Jeb make a grab for it. The Indian quickly threw Jeb off, making a move for the knife himself. Jeb quickly pounced again, and they rolled one way then the other, but neither had the knife. Jeb came to his feet first, and as the Indian was coming to his feet, Jeb let go with a haymaker, catching the Indian on the left side of the jaw. The Indian then sprawled backwards and when he hit the ground, he hit his head on a large rock and went limp. Jeb jumped on him, raising his head by the hair, only to see blood on the back of his head. Jeb then realized the fight was over.

He stood on rubbery legs, but looked around to see if there was more danger to be aware of. When he was sure there wasn't, he went down on one knee, breathing hard. He stayed there for a few minutes, catching his wind. He went to his horse and mounted, then rode back to the mining district. When he got there, he had fully restored his wind. He rode up to where Lieutenant Brentwood was sitting in his camp chair.

The lieutenant had seen Jeb riding back, but did not rise from his chair. He looked up at Jeb and asked, "what happened to you? You look a mess."

"Me and a Pawnee Indian had at each other."

"And, you won, huh?"

Jeb replied, "I'm here, ain't I?"

Lieutenant Brentwood chuckled at that, then said, "I didn't think you'd be coming back. Let me buy you a cup of coffee. Come, lite and take a load off. They must feel rather heavy right about now."

"Naw," Jeb answered. "Think I'll sit here a spell. I have a strange feelin' that if I step down, I'll continue right to the ground."

"Could be that's what you need, Jeb. Rest." Motioning with a backwards thumb, "I have a cot you can use if you want."

Jeb chuckled, then said, "no thanks. I'm just fine right where I am."

"Humph!" Lieutenant Brentwood replied. "Suit yourself."

"Thank you. I will."

Lieutenant Brentwood then went back to writing his troop report. After a few minutes, Jeb dismounted and stood next to him. He looked at Jeb and asked, "you think the Pawnee will be back?"

"No," Jeb answered. "They've been hurt and hurt bad. They won't be back."

"And, that lone Indian?" the lieutenant asked.

Jeb turned to the lieutenant, then said, "don't know."

Lieutenant Brentwood breathed in deeply, then exhaling, said, "I hope you're right, Winslow. I sure hope you're right."

"I'm only human. I do make mistakes, ya know."

"Mistakes, Winslow, takes lives," he replied. "I, we can't afford mistakes."

Jeb chuckled, then said, "yet, they still are made, Lieutenant, by the best of men."

Lieutenant Brentwood sighed, then said, "unfortunately, Winslow, they do at the cost of few, or many lives."

***

At Camp Nelson, Major Ivers had requested Lieutenant Hollis to his office. When the lieutenant arrived, he stood in front of the desk, saluted the major and said, "Lieutenant Hollis, reporting as ordered, Sir."

Major Ivers was standing over by the window to the left of his desk, and said, "stand at ease, Lieutenant."

"Yes, Sir. Thank you, Sir."

Major Ivers walked to his desk and seated himself, then looked up at Lieutenant Hollis. "I want you to take your troop and relieve Lieutenant Brentwood at the Copper Penny Mining District, Lieutenant. You'll leave around noon tomorrow. You are to stay until you are relieved. Is that understood, Lieutenant?"

"Yes, Sir. Understood, Sir."

"Prepare for your departure, Lieutenant."

Lieutenant Hollis replied, "Yes, Sir. Thank you, Sir."

Major Ivers then said, "that will be all, Lieutenant, and take what's his name? Arapoosh? Take him with you as scout."

As Lieutenant Hollis saluted Major Ivers, he said, "yes, Sir, I will. Thank you, Sir."

Without waiting for a return salute, Lieutenant Hollis turned and left the office, closing the door behind him.

Major Ivers shook his head slightly, then said, "I must get out more often."

Chapter Seven

Jeeb

Lieutenant Landers and his troop entered Camp Nelson the worse for wear. All ragged and disheveled from their journey to and from Alpine Meadows in the Big Horn Mountains, and their brush with the Blackfeet attacking a stage coach on the flatlands. He turned to Sergeant Wallace. "walk your mounts for thirty minutes, Sergeant, before you stable them."

"Yes, Sir."

The lieutenant stepped down and tethered his horse at the hitching rack as Major Ivers came from headquarters, and Linda Porter came running to him from the hospital. When she came within a few feet of him, she yelled, "Paul! Paul!" He turned to her as she plowed into him, burying her head against his chest and wrapping her arms around him, almost knocking him off balance. Major Ivers stood staring at them with a dead pan look.

He then shoved Linda aside as he saluted Major Ivers. "Sorry, Major."

Major Ivers replied, "that's quite all right, Lieutenant. Miss Porter and I were worried for the same reasons."

Lieutenant Landers looked confused, then said, "Sir?"

"Long story, Lieutenant. Miss Porter can explain later, but right now, I have to say, it's good to have you back."

Linda turned to the major. "Major?"

"Oh, excuse me, Miss Porter."

Lieutenant Landers smiled as Linda again buried her head in his chest and wrapped her arms around him."

Major Ivers, then said, "oh, Lieutenant, when the formalities have ended, meet me in my office, if you would please, but don't make those formalities last too long. You have men watching."

Lieutenant Landers replied, "yes, Sir. I mean, no, Sir."

Major Ivers chuckled, then said, "Which ever one works, Lieutenant."

Just then, Paul leaned down and kissed Linda, and she melted in his arms.

Major Ivers went to turn from them, but hesitated a second or two just to watch. As if mesmerized, he just stared. Then, with raised eyebrows, he said, "yes. Well." He then turned and went back into headquarters, smiling as he did so.

Linda raised her head to look at Paul, then said, "I was so worried for you, Paul. I missed you so much, it hurts."

Paul brushed her hair with his hand. "I missed you, too, Linda. This was a rough patrol, but now, I'm back. *And*, I must go see Major Ivers and inform him of what we found on that patrol. We can renew our being together later, but..."

Linda lowered her head. "I'm sorry. I'm getting in the way of your duty, aren't I?"

Paul lifted her head with his hand, smiled, then said, "a welcomed distraction, Linda, as always." He went to kiss her again, but he eyed those around him, who were staring at them with envy. Linda, herself, then eyed those who were looking at them with envy, and smiled unconsciously. "We must be discreet, Linda, especially in front of the men." Linda agreed. Then, they parted as Lieutenant Landers went into headquarters and the major's office.

When he entered the office, he stood in front of the desk. "Sorry, Sir. It took a little longer than it should have, delaying my report."

Major Ivers replied, "Yes, it did, Lieutenant, but it was quite understandable, this time. I'm not so sure I wouldn't have done the same thing in your boots, but let's get down to business."

"Yes, Sir."

Major Ivers, then asked, "well, Lieutenant, what did you find at Alpine Meadows?" He sat and listened to the lieutenant's report, hanging on every word. When Lieutenant Landers ended his report, he said, "and, you say these Indians were Blackfeet who laid waste to the settlement, and had attacked the stage?"

"Yes, Sir."

Major Ivers rose from his chair, then went to the window, looking out. Without turning to Lieutenant Landers, he said, "we need reinforcements, Lieutenant." Turning to the lieutenant, "we need more men at this post, but unfortunately, they are unavailable just now."

Lieutenant Landers suggested, "we could get the settlers to lend a hand, Major."

Major Ivers answered, "that's a good idea, Lieutenant, but they are not Army, and neither are they under my direct command."

"That's true, Sir, but they have a stake in this as well, Sir. Their very lives are at stake. We could use a voluntary command, as it were, like the state militia."

Major Ivers smiled, then said, "very good, Lieutenant. Very good. I do like your idea. I do." He rubbed his chin, then said, "a state militia, huh? Instead of making Camp Nelson a fort, we can apply to the Army to make Camp Nelson a state militia headquarters and have camps all over the territory. That is a very good idea, Lieutenant. I will make a note of this and send it forward to the Army department for approval by the Secretary of Defense."

Lieutenant Landers smiled widely, then said, "thank you, Sir."

Major Ivers, then said, "I will personally make sure that the Army department knows this was your idea, Lieutenant." He chuckled, then said, "you just might wind up with a promotion, and a commendation, to boot."

Lieutenant Landers was still smiling widely, then asked, "you really think so, Major?"

"Stranger things have happened, Lieutenant. Yes, Sir, stranger things have happened." He walked back over to the window, rubbing the back of his neck in thought. He turned back and said, "damn, Lieutenant, I wish I had thought of that myself."

Beaming with pride, Lieutenant Landers replied, "Yes, Sir."

"I will make out the proper paperwork and have it in the mail tomorrow, barring any delays, and we should know something, hopefully, by the end of the month. That, Sir, was an excellent idea." Lieutenant Landers stood proud of himself. "That was an excellent report, as well, Lieutenant. Have it in writing by day's end, Lieutenant. That will be all."

Lieutenant Landers saluted the major. "Yes, Sir. Thank you, Sir." This time, Major Ivers returned the salute and Lieutenant Landers turned and left the office.

Major Ivers searched the drawers of his desk, then befuddled in his search, he yelled to the duty sergeant, "Sergeant Daniels, do you have a copy of the form #13-70.2 in there? I can't seem to find one in here," as he continued his search.

The major was mumbling to himself as Sergeant Daniels brought in the form. "Here's the form you're lookin' for, Major."

As Sergeant Daniels handed the form to him, the major said, "Thank you, Sergeant."

"You're welcome, Sir. Anything else, Major?"

Disgusted with himself, the major replied, "no, that'll be all, Sergeant."

"Yes, Sir."

As the sergeant turned and went to the door, the major said, "there is one thing, Sergeant."

"Yes, Sir?"

"Make sure I'm not disturbed for the next hour, unless it is an emergency."

"Yes, Sir."

The major then pointed to the door. "And close my door."

***

Linda met Paul as he came from headquarters, then they rushed away to her temporary quarters. Once inside and behind closed doors, they clung to each other, whispering their love for each other. They kissed longingly. Then breaking their kiss, she rested her head on his chest. Then, just above a whisper, she said, "I love you, Paul. I don't know what I'd do if I was to lose you. Die of a broken heart, I guess."

Paul whiffed the sweet aroma of her perfume and the fragrance of her hair, then spoke into the top of her head, asking, "and, what makes you think you'd lose me, Linda?"

With Paul's arms wrapped around her, she tilted back from him, saying, "your death, for one."

"My death?" Paul asked, confused. "I know there's that possibility, Linda, but..."

Breaking from his embrace, Linda walked a few feet from him, turned, then said, "Yes, Paul. Your death." Paul stood staring at her, not knowing what to say, then she said, "when you left for your patrol, it kept ringing in my ears, this may be the last time I see you, alive, that is."

"Linda, you must understand."

"There's only two things I understand, Paul. You're a Lieutenant in the Cavalry and must do your duty and follow orders. The other is, I love you with every fiber in my body, and I want us to live a happy, glorious life together and have many children together. But..."

"But, what, Linda?"

Linda answered, "The what is, what if you come back dead from one of your patrols? We can't live a happy, glorious life together if you're dead, Paul."

Paul's shoulders sank as if in defeat. He looked at Linda longingly, then in tenderness he said, "you shouldn't have come here, Linda. I have enough stress and knowing how you feel now just adds to it."

Linda almost shouted, "I now cause you stress? I cause you stress? Is that what you're saying?"

Paul turned his eyes from her, then said, "yes. You're causing me to choose between you and my duty, and that is causing me stress." He turned back to her. "I love the Army, and I love you, Linda, very much."

Linda replied, "you love me, but not as much as you love the Army. Is that it?"

Paul threw both hands in the air, then asked, "how can I answer that Linda? Why can't I love you and the Army both as much at the same time?"

Linda shouted, "because the Army will probably get you killed!" She turned from him, sobbing into her hands thrust up to her face.

Paul replied, "you knew that could happen when we got together, Linda. I can't apologize my being an officer in the US Army."

"I'm not asking you to apologize, Paul."

"No, you're not. You're just wanting me to resign my commission and go off with you and live happily ever after."

Linda lovingly asked, "and, what's wrong with that? Paul, listen..."

Paul replied, angrily, "I've had all the listening I can take from you, Linda. First, you're all lovey-dovey when I get back, then you're telling me you worry when I'm gone, then you're all lovey-dovey with me when I do get back, and now, you want me to resign my commission, and go off and live some fairy tale. Life doesn't work that way, Linda. You either accept me as an officer in the Army, or..."

Linda turned quickly, asking, "Or, what, Paul?"

"Or," Paul hesitated, then said, "or, it's over between us. This stress is getting to be too much. I love you, but we can't go on like this. Not no more. I just can't."

Turning from him, she said, "then, it's over, Paul. We have nothing more to say to each other. Goodbye, Paul."

Paul stood in disbelief, then said, "I'll talk to the major and arrange for your immediate return to New York. When that will be, I wouldn't know." He turned and went to the door. Opening it, he turned back and said, "Goodbye, Linda." With that said, he closed the door behind him.

Linda quickly turned, with tears in her eyes, and whispered, "Paul?" staring at a closed door.

***

The following afternoon, Lieutenant Brentwood was sitting in his camp chair writing his troop report when Jeb came riding in with Lieutenant Hollis, Arapoosh and his troop. Standing to his feet, he placed his report in his chair. As they rode up to him, Lieutenant Hollis shouted, "Troop! Halt!"

Then, Jeb said, "Look here who I found, Lieutenant."

Lieutenant Brentwood replied, "I see, Winslow." He turned to Lieutenant Hollis, saying, "Welcome to the Copper Penny Mining District, Les."

Lieutenant Lester Hollis stepped down from the saddle and said, "I heard of this place, Jirus, but this is the first time ever being here. Any trouble?"

Lieutenant Brentwood answered, "Some, wouldn't you say, Winslow?"

"I would indeed, Lieutenant. I would indeed."

Lieutenant Hollis asked, "Oh? Sioux?"

Jeb replied, "no. Pawnee, Lieutenant."

Arapoosh then said, "Pawnee? You sure, Jeeb?"

"As sure as you're born, Arapoosh."

Lieutenant Brentwood chuckled, then asked, "Jeeb? Did I hear him call you, Jeeb, Winslow?"

Jeb scrunched up his face as he stepped down from the saddle, then said, "yeah, he calls me Jeeb, but that's because he can't say Jeb correctly."

Still chuckling, Lieutenant Brentwood said, "I have just found a new name for you, Jeb. Hey, Jeeb."

"Very funny, Lieutenant. Very funny. Ha, ha, ha." That just caused Lieutenant Brentwood to laugh uproariously. Jeb turned to Arapoosh, saying, "Now, see what you started?"

Laughing down to a chuckle, Lieutenant Brentwood turned to Lieutenant Hollis and said, "it's all yours, Les. Take care of the place, will you?"

"Like it was my own, Jirus," Lieutenant Hollis answered.

Lieutenant Brentwood said, "well, Jeeb, I think it's time we're going home."

"Keep it up, Lieutenant. Just keep it up." Jeb turned to Arapoosh with a curl of the lip. Arapoosh just shrugged his shoulders.

Lieutenant Brentwood turned to Sergeant Bracken. "Sergeant, assemble the men and have them ready to ride. We're going home."

Sergeant Bracken replied, "yes, Sir, Lieutenant." He turned from the lieutenant, and walking away, started barking commands. Within fifteen minutes, the troop was ready to ride for Camp Nelson.

When the troopers were sitting their horses ready to go, Lieutenant Brentwood smiled at Lieutenant Hollis, then said, "you'll be alright, Les, and when you ain't, don't forget to duck."

Lieutenant Hollis smiled back, then replied, "sage advice, Jirus. Sage advice."

Then, looking back over his shoulder, Lieutenant Brentwood yelled, "Troop! Forward! Ho!"

Lieutenant Hollis stood, watching as Lieutenant Brentwood and his troop rode away, back to Camp Nelson. Arapoosh, then stepped up onto his pony and rode away to scout for Lieutenant Hollis and the men at the Copper Penny Mining District. Lieutenant Hollis sat in the camp chair, Lieutenant Brentwood left behind, and began to write his obligatory troop report of that day.

***

The Sioux, Arapaho, Cheyenne, Fox, Ute, Pawnee, Kiowa, Arikara, and the Blackfeet were the many dangers of frontier life in Wyoming, but the Sioux and the Cheyenne were the worst of the lot. The Wind River Campaign, along the many miles of that river, and in the valley of the warm winds, the Sioux uprising had met head on. Since the Laramie Treaty of 1851, warlike conditions existed between the warring factions of the Sioux and the US Army. Even when the treaty was signed and sealed, the white man encroached on Indian land even before the ink had dried on the paper. Raids and battles with the Sioux and Cheyenne continued, which included the massacre at Wounded Knee in 1890.

Treaty after treaty was broken by the white man, even though the Indians had kept those treaties.

As to Camp Nelson? The Army department approved the idea Lieutenant Landers had suggested and Camp Nelson became the headquarters of the state militia. He was promoted to Captain, with a commendation. As to him and Linda Porter, Linda was put on a stage and headed for Cheyenne, Wyoming to catch a train back to New York. The two had parted ways.

Major Ivers was transferred to a post more to his experience, and lo and behold, he sent for his wife, and they had a happy reunion. Nate Markenson was killed in the battle of Cheyenne Pass.

Arapoosh, the Crow scout, was killed in an ambush by the Sioux in 1870 near Casper, Wyoming.

As to Tobias Canfield, he was wounded in a raid in the valley of the warm winds where he was traveling on his way to Beaver Falls with all manner of furs, beaver pelts. He later died of his wound in 1871.

Jeb Winslow died at the ripe old age of 75, where he lived on Casper Mountain, near Casper, Wyoming. He died peacefully in his sleep. He had not married and had almost nothing to leave, but a memory. A memory to those who knew and loved him for the stories he told of the wild and woolly past. His stories fascinated and entertained the young with his backwoods manner, his tall tales and the yarns he told. He had become almost a legend while he was still alive. He was recognized right up there with Buffalo Bill Cody and Wild Bill Hickock, and he felt somewhat proud to be known in that kind of company. His funeral was a lavish one, even though he had hardly no money. The best memory of Jeb Winslow was the Wind River Campaign, and his exploits there.